Sunrise over Paris

Carolyn Eychenne

PEPITAGA

Press

SUNRISE OVER PARIS

Copyright © 2020 by Carolyn Eychenne.

For information contact :

Pepitaga Press

https://www.pepitagapress.com

Carolyn Eychenne

https://www.carolyneychenne.com

Cover design by Ashley Santoro

Book formatting template by Derek Murphy of Creativindie Design

ISBN: 978-2-9575528-0-1

First Edition: 2020

10 9 8 7 6 5 4 3 2 1

Part I

*"Le marriage est comme le restaurant,
à peine servi on regarde dans l'assiette
du voisin."*
--Sacha Guitry

Marriage is like eating out.
Almost as soon as your meal arrives
you start looking at the meals on the
next table.

1

The discovery

IT WAS SHOCKING how simple it was for her world to collapse. Stacey was in bed, reading, as she usually did before going to sleep. She didn't remember what the novel was, something easy to relax with at the end of the day. Jean lay next to her, a little space between them, just enough so she didn't bump him when she turned pages. He read emails, as he often did. There was silence as each one read, but a companionable silence, the quiet of people who know each other well and are confident in one another's presence. All was well. Or reasonably well.

And then, suddenly, it wasn't.

Between chapters, Stacey happened to glance over at her husband's tablet. Why? She'd never know. She glanced over, saw the beginning word, just one word, Chéri, and knew. She knew why Jean had felt so distant, why he had become critical of her when he had previously been supportive, why he had stopped inviting her to Paris for date night and started watching his weight and no longer ate her gratin dauphinois.

She felt the wind knocked out of her, like taking a sucker punch to the gut. Breathing just wasn't possible right away, which made a yoga cleansing breath a non-starter. She said nothing, just lay there, prostrate. Her mind recovered before her breath did. Damn! She couldn't read the rest of the email. It was no longer visible since Jean had continued on to the next email in his inbox, but the list of senders was still visible on the far left of his tablet. Carefully, moving only her eyes, she searched the list of senders, a little above the one that was highlighted. A woman's name. Berenice Jaunatre. Surrounded by communications from Jean's bank, his alumni club, his car retailer, was one single email from a private account in a woman's name.

Le salaud! The bastard!

Her eyes had come back to the page in front of her, but she was having a hard time focusing. Her breath came back, all at once. She gasped for air. Jean looked over at her, inquiringly, then looked back at his emails. Stacey didn't dare look back, didn't dare speak. Her body was immobile, while her mind raced. It imitated an Olympic runner, sprinting from hurdle to hurdle, but one who just couldn't stop after 100-yards, 200-yards, 10,000 meters, the marathon.

How could he? When did they meet? Who was she? What was she like? These thoughts made sleep impossible and the night very long. As the hours dragged on, she realized that listening to Jean sleep peacefully was almost as devastating as his infidelity.

Why should he sleep when she couldn't? It was all his fault. She should confront him. She should deprive him of sleep until he confessed. She should...

More than anything, she should have known. There were signs, even at dinner the night before.

2

Dinnertime

INNERTIME WAS THE ONE moment of the day when the entire family reunited, to break bread together, share their day, discuss current events, expound on their dreams and desires. Every day Stacey, wife and mom, spent the better part of an hour preparing a home-cooked meal (no ready meals in this house) with fresh vegetables, free range chicken or hormone-free meat, a bubbly cobbler or fruit pie out of the oven just in time for dessert. Dinner was the glue that kept this family, and all families, together.

She looked across the table at her loved ones: her husband Jean, her son David and daughter Laura, 15 and 17, although in her heart Stacey still saw the little girl and boy they once had been.

Her daughter Laura wore only red and black, at the same time, often in ways her mother didn't understand. Those red and black striped knee socks, no, not "knee" socks since they covered half the thigh and stopped just low enough to expose an inch or two of bare flesh below the red and black plaid mini-skirt. Which raised another question: when did it become OK to wear stripes with plaid? And when did red and black start going together? *If only that were all*, she thought, as she eyed the make-up, considering it more of a slash job than merely make-up, besmeared over what was, when freshly washed, a lovely face. The French had a saying, "*maquillée comme une voiture volée.*" Painted like a stolen car. That pretty much described her daughter this evening.

The clothes, the make-up, the piercings. And the earphones, little bitty ear buds, jammed squarely in each ear, buzzing intently with a music which was just as aggressive as her outfit. The entire ensemble was calculated to say "Don't ask me how school went today." No, not to say, to scream, "DON'T ASK ME..."

Stacey sighed, knowing the uselessness of any

conversational foray in that direction. She looked over at her son David, a gentle soul, dressed more normally in jeans and a t-shirt. As much as his sister's accoutrement was calculated and painstakingly executed, his was *negligé*, unkempt. Too much so. Those jeans and t-shirt were the same ones as yesterday and, if memory served, the day before that as well. Hair unbrushed; there was a good chance it was unwashed too. Day-old beard. Or, it would be a day-old beard if he were older and the beard, more hardy. Next to his plate lay his tablet with its mini-keyboard. Eyes glued to the screen, he typed in something with a gun-burst of tap-tapping, distractedly took a forkful of meat before snorting at whatever just appeared on his screen and fired off another round of key-rattling. Whatever was happening on that screen was a thousand times more real to him than the people sitting around the table. She probably could have filled his plate with sawdust and set it on fire without him noticing the difference.

She took a deep breath and let it out slowly, trying to expel the negative thoughts with the air, as she learned in yoga class. A cleansing breath, the instructor had said. Properly cleansed, she turned to her husband Jean. "Would you like another piece of gratin?" she asked, holding the serving spoon over the baking dish in readiness. In expectancy. She knew how much he liked her *gratin dauphinois,* thin slices of potato layered in a cream sauce, baked until the potatoes practically melted and the top became a browned crust. Things had been tense between them recently, she didn't know why, so she had made the dish as a sort of peace offering. He scowled at her, then at the potatoes, at her readiness to appease him.

"No. That's really the trouble with you," he said. "You keep making all this heavy stuff. I need to lose some of this waistline. Do you have any more salad?" Both of them looked at the empty salad bowl, then looked up at one another, his eyes with a certain challenge in them.

She looked away. "Sure, let me prepare some more." She got up, leaving her own plate half eaten, to wash and prepare more greens. Angry. Thinking, *Any fool could have seen the bowl was empty. That gratin took me ages.*

If dinner was the glue, the family was coming unstuck.

The evening did not improve as it moved on.

Au contraire, Stacey thought.

3

The day after

THE NEXT MORNING, Stacey got up in a fog, a twinge of migraine from lack of sleep. She downed an espresso, then another, as if she were doing shots, then felt lucid enough to prepare breakfast for the family, while Jean and the kids got ready.

Usually the kids ate fast and left for school, which would give her a moment to confront Jean with what she had seen the night before. Maybe she should have another coffee. It might help her discuss this civilly.

All three came downstairs at the same time. Jean helped himself to coffee and a piece of fruit, which annoyed Stacey. *He must still be worried about his waistline*, she thought, then checked herself. *If you want this to go well, you'd better hold your temper.*

Just then, Laura and David both reached for the last croissant at the same time.

"That's mine," Laura said.

"No, it's mine. You already had yours," David answered.

"You did, too. I saw you."

"But I'm a guy. I don't have to worry about getting fat like you do."

"What the f**k?"

"Language," Stacey interrupted.

"Stop shouting," Jean said.

"He keeps taking more than his share," Laura said to her father. Then, to her brother, "I do way more sports than you, so if someone should be worried about his weight, it's doughboy over there."

The kids continued their bickering, each one pulling on the end of the croissant until it tore in two. It would have been funny if their animosity wasn't so clear, and if their loud voices weren't making Stacey's headache worse.

Stacey grabbed the croissant pieces from both of them,

slamming down baguettes in front of each.

"The croissant is mine," she said. "I haven't eaten yet."

The kids started arguing once more. Jean got up from the table, giving Stacey a quick peck on the forehead.

"Gotta run," he said. "I've got an early meeting."

He left.

And Stacey's hopes to confront him, to have a civil conversation about the affair, went right out the door with him.

She got up, poured herself a coffee and took it upstairs, away from her bickering kids. They'd work it out- - or not. They'd get to school on time—or not. Right then, she just couldn't worry about that.

4

The Seine

STACEY LOOKED AT the clock. Only 9 a.m. and she was already tired. Jean was gone. The kids were gone. After her sleepless night, the kids' fight, and the non-conversation with Jean this morning, she was tired. And frustrated. And angry. And ...

She plopped down on the sofa, turned on the TV, and channel surfed, flipping through channel after channel, looking for something to distract her, and only found love story after love story. Worse was some reality TV show about picking the best bridal gown. Those brides-to-be were lucky their show wasn't interactive or she would give them a dose of reality! She snapped off the TV in disgust.

She walked over to her bookshelves, searched a moment, and found what she was looking for, *La Femme Rompue, The Broken Woman,* by Simone de Beauvoir, wife of Jean Paul Sartre and one of France's leading 20th century authors in her own right. This had been assigned reading in 3rd year French class, an odd choice to put in the hands of twenty- year-olds. At the time she had struggled to read the book, a story of infidelity and its effect on the main character Monique, only to conclude, "Whiner."

But that was youth. The young could be harsh in their judgments, not having lived enough to be forced to make compromises in their lives and concessions in their ideals. Now, at fifty, Stacey thought she would revisit the short novel, hoping it would tell her what she should do now, because she didn't know. She fixed herself a nice hot *café au lait,* settled down on the sofa and read. And read and read. And cried. She was especially moved when she came to this passage in the heroine's words:

"My life behind me has completely collapsed, as in those earthquakes where the soil devours itself; it swallows itself behind your back as you flee. There is no return. The house disappeared, the village, the whole valley. Even if you survive, nothing remains, not even the place you occupied on this earth."

That was exactly how she felt! Long ago, the author had found just the right words, just the right tone, to express what Stacey was feeling now.

She read on, a feeling of exasperation growing until she threw the book down. Thirty years ago, she had been right. Monique was a whiner.

She turned the TV back on. Video on demand. Clicking here and there, "It's got to be here somewhere," she muttered to herself. Ah, there it was. *The Good Wife*. She watched an episode or three, crying with Alicia's humiliation, sympathizing with her pain, and admiring her strength. Stacey knew she wasn't a whiner, like Monique, *La Femme Rompue*. She was made of more solid stuff. Watching the series, she realized that she wasn't nearly as solid as "Saint Alicia" in *The Good Wife*, either.

She clicked off the TV and went back to her bookshelves, still hoping to find a clue that would tell her what to do. She studied the spines, touching a book here or there, before pulling one out. Nina Killham, *How to Cook a Tart*. Now that was a fun story! Jasmine March, the main character, was a foodie, like Stacey. Jasmine discovered her husband was cheating on her, again like Stacey, and struck back... by giving a cooking lesson to the mistress. The mistress was found dead in Jasmine's kitchen. Various characters hid the body, some together, some individually, which led to surprises – and body parts—popping up where you least expected them. A rollicking good story, very *noir*, but not helpful to Stacey; it wasn't a great idea to react to her husband's infidelity by making a *pâté-en-croûte* out of the Jezebel's head.

She put the book back in place, thought for a moment, then went to pick up her keys. Sometimes, when she was in a funk, going for a walk helped. Stacey often walked along the banks of the Seine, browsing at the *bouquinistes*, the book vendors along the river, much like Hemingway had done, looking at the boats, especially the "fly boats" with all the tourists, cruising up and down the river. The French had two words for river: *rivière* and *fleuve*. A *fleuve* flowed into the sea. The *rivière*, on the other hand, flowed into a *fleuve*. What did the Seine flow into? She had never learned enough geography to know which word to use.

Stacey parked near Notre Dame, went to the river bank, and headed west, thinking she would walk to Trocadero, cross the bridge to the Eiffel Tower and back to Saint Michel on the other bank. It was quite a ways, but it would do her good. She had gone only a block when she saw her first couple, a "happy loving couple" as Joe Jackson sang. The young woman was sitting on the wall overlooking the Seine. Her boyfriend leaned in to kiss her. They looked very happy, very much in love.

Stacey turned her head away.

Their happiness stung like a slap in the face. She had been in love like that, once.

She and Jean both. She had come to France to study abroad and visited Paris on spring break with other American girls in her program. Her friends were all very earnest, having studied French for many years, having dreamed of France for so long that they had list after list of places to see and things to do. Stacey tagged along, *mettant ses pieds sous la table*, just putting her feet under the table, as the French say to describe someone who does nothing to prepare.

Was it laziness? Her Californian laid-back nature? She didn't know, but the fact that Stacey wasn't bent over the guide books all the time meant that she was looking at what was going on around her, particularly at the cute French guy she first noticed at the *Orangerie* and later at a café. He was handsome, but there was something else she couldn't put her finger on, something that thrilled her. She smiled. He smiled back and, as Stacey and her friends got up to visit the next museum, he came over and asked if he could take her to dinner that evening.

She had said yes. They had gone to dinner, and they had kissed, just like that young couple over by the Seine.

She sighed and walked on, still hoping the Seine would work its magic.

Was it the sunshine? The time of year? Some sort of communist plot? It seemed like there was a happy loving couple at every street corner, there to taunt her, to remind her of her own unhappiness. She continued walking, determined to make exercise and endorphins do their job, until she got to the *Pont des Arts*.

All those padlocks, snapped shut on the chain link of the bridge, symbolizing the vows made by all those lovers, come to Paris as if on a pilgrimage to *l'amour*. The sun reflected off the metal locks, blinding her with their brilliance. And there! Another couple, kissing, helping one another pass the shackle through the chain link, snapping the lock closed, throwing the key in the Seine, then embracing once again.

Enough already! Vanquished, Stacey turned back. She crossed the street to walk next to the shops, away from the lovers, away from the Seine which had failed her. Somehow, the Seine's betrayal hurt as much as her husband's.

5

Mediocrity and daube

NOSTALGIA IS TREACHEROUS, thought Stacey. Thinking about how she and Jean had met led Stacey to think about her childhood, her teens years, university, her wild dreams, her dashed hopes.

When Stacey was a little girl, she'd had grand dreams. Around 12, Stacey decided she would become a writer. Or, should she say, Writer? Her texts would be Important. Literature. The capital L being important here. Only several years later did she learn the phrase to express what she had felt so keenly: she would write the next Great American Novel.

High school brought new ideas of law school, becoming a lawyer and really changing people's lives. Making a difference. Stacey could become the first woman Supreme Court Justice. Thanks Sandra Day for wrecking that dream.

In the meantime, of course, she went to college, worked in law offices during vacations, got enough firsthand experience to decide law was not for her, and wandered over to France to spend her junior year abroad, loved it, and returned after graduation to teach English. That one year turned into thirty, teaching turned into ad sales, which was the direct opposite of "really making a difference." The flirting with Jean turned into love. They got married, had kids, and she quit work to dedicate herself to her family.

The results were... mixed, at best. Her children were reasonably good people but her dark mood led her to believe they neither truly liked nor respected her. Her husband, she had just learned, was cheating on her. The hurt, the betrayal... being made a cliché!

It was all so ... mediocre.

It wasn't as if you wake up one morning and decide you wanted to be mediocre. After all, mediocrity was not a goal. More like a reality that you are forced to admit, sometimes little by little, sometimes, like a slap in the face, as she learned and then realized the full extent of her husband's betrayal.

There was only one thing to do. Every now and then, when she felt down, when she felt blah, when she felt mediocre and needed to pull herself out of it, Stacey would pull out the recipe.

Daube referred to the type of dish, a sort of stew, similar to a *bourguignon*. Stacey had eaten it the first time she came to France.

A student on a college exchange program, she rented a room with Mademoiselle Geoffroy. The school she attended had arranged for her to have a room in Mademoiselle Geoffroy's apartment, with breakfast and dinner during the week. Mademoiselle Geoffroy, eighty years old, a devout Catholic attending mass every day (Stacey hadn't even known that they hold mass every day), was an excellent cook, traditional French cuisine all the way. The lodger the preceding semester was vegetarian, which was difficult for Mademoiselle Geoffroy even to comprehend, let alone cook for.

Mademoiselle Geoffroy loved to cook; Stacey loved to eat, so the two got along. A match made in heaven.

Mademoiselle Geoffroy often made *omelette aux*

épinards, spinach omelet, as a starter. Stacey didn't like spinach but learned that, if there were any leftovers, she would see them again the next day, reheated in a toaster oven so that the top was a carbonized crust. While spinach omelet was bad, burned spinach omelet was even worse, so Stacey started eating the entire thing the first time around. Only after a few months did she realize that Mademoiselle Geoffroy was serving the spinach omelet more and more often, so that it became a weekly item, once even twice in the same week. When Stacey asked her why, Mademoiselle Geoffroy answered "Because you like it so much."

Spinach omelet had become her Catch-22.

Another of Mademoiselle Geoffroy's regular dishes was a *daube.* Pieces of meat in a heavy wine sauce, cooked so long that the meat practically melted with each mouthful. Heaven. Nothing in Stacey's eighteen years in California had prepared her for such a heady rush of flavors. It was the culinary equivalent of giving a Maserati to a kid used to a tricycle.

The first time she tasted this manna, Stacey asked Mademoiselle Geoffroy "Is this beef?"

"No."

"Is this mutton?"

"No."

"Is this pork?"

"No."

"Is this chicken?" Stacey knew this couldn't be chicken, but wanted to cover all the bases.

"No."

Coming to the limits of her French vocabulary, Stacey asked "Well, what is it?"

"Meat."

"Meat?"

"Yes, meat."

She accepted that, thinking that one day she would learn more vocabulary and so would learn what the mysterious ingredient was.

Mademoiselle Geoffroy served this dish, twice a month, for the entire semester the two lived together. At the end of the semester, in Stacey's French civilization class, the professor described the *boucherie chevaline*. Stacey had passed in front of these shops in the city of Aix, a big storefront, a door, a horse's head much like a hunter's trophy hanging over the door. She would glance in, see the pieces of meat in the glass counters, and not think any further about it. Only during class that day did she learn that the horse's head was product marketing; the rest of the horse lay in that glass showcase, being sold as dinner.

A typical way to serve horsemeat? In a *daube*. As the professor described the dish, Stacey realized that this was what she had been eating, every two weeks, for the last four months. Horrified, she raced home to Mademoiselle Geoffroy. She described the dish to her and asked "Is it horse?"

Mademoiselle Geoffroy sighed, as if she had been through this time and time again with her American student lodgers. "Yes, it's horse. Do you want me to stop making it?"

Stacey answered slowly, thinking it through before speaking.

"No, it's OK. I've liked it for four months, there is no reason that I should stop liking it today." That day, she rose in Mademoiselle Geoffroy's esteem.

Thinking about Mademoiselle Geoffroy led Stacey to think about the challenges of making a life in France in those early years. Maybe because she was still mastering the language back then, a lot of her difficulties were linguistic. Like saying "*non*," instead of "no." There was, actually, a difference.

Or, hushing a child, a French person would say "*chhhut!*" instead of the American "shhhhh." That "t" on the end gave it a harshness and finality which made the kid obey. When someone offered you something to eat and you wanted it, you said "*merci*." When someone offered you something and you did not want it, you also said "*merci.*" It had taken Stacey years to hear the difference in the inflections let alone reproduce them. This had resulted in many unwanted second helpings.

What about "*ce n'est pas mal ?* " Literally, "it's not bad." In the mouth of a Frenchman, this meant the opposite. It was good, perhaps even great, but something in the culture kept them from saying so directly or with too much enthusiasm.

The same circuitous thinking was behind "*ce n'est pas impossible,*" it's not impossible, which meant "yes, we can do that."

Of course, even the French realized this tendency to complicate things. The national proverb was "*Pourquoi faire simple quand on peut faire compliqué ?*" why do things simply when you can make them complicated? This pretty much summed up French cuisine, literature, cinema...

Stacey pulled herself from these musings, telling herself *I must pay attention*! Pay attention—that's another one. In English, the verb was pay, like you pay money, which suggests that you expect something in return, in this case, success in her recipe. In French, attention was something you do or make, "*faire attention.*" Did this mean there was no payback? That the French "made" attention just for the hell of it? Stacey loved the French people but wasn't convinced that altruism was one of their strong points.

She pulled herself from these thoughts yet again to concentrate fully on preparing her *daube*.

The recipe Stacey used was created by Joel Robuchon, one of France's finest, who closed every episode of his TV show with "*Bon appétit*, of course." Buy top-notch ingredients. A good mutton instead of horse meat. Take the time to reduce the wine. Don't hurry when you seared the meat. Don't crowd the pieces, so that you locked in the juices, ensuring a tender result. Pre-cook the mushrooms on high, listening to them "scream" in the pan. You made the mushrooms scream not because you were a sadist but because this really did change the flavor of the mushrooms and was worth the extra effort.

For the next three hours, Stacey performed each step conscientiously, paying attention to the details, making each item just right before going on to the next step. A culinary mindfulness exercise. The result was perfection: juicy morsels of lamb melting in her mouth, pieces of mushroom in counter-point to the meat offering more resistance between the teeth, the unctuous gravy—no, she didn't like the word 'gravy' with its connotations of Thanksgiving leftovers or the lowly chicken-fried steak. This was something altogether more noble, more complex, ingredients coming together to create a symphony of flavors.

Stacey served the *daube* with tagliatelle, the traditionalist's accompaniment, and watched her family as they ate. It was one of those rare moments when they all slowed down. They concentrated on what they were eating. They savored. They discussed the different flavors in the dish. They discussed other great meals they had eaten together. And Jean didn't worry about his waistline.

She hadn't written the Great American Novel, she hadn't created jurisprudence in the Supreme Court, but she had made an excellent *daube*. She had nourished her family and created a space for sharing, loving and laughing. For the space of an evening, Stacey felt like excellence incarnate.

6

Coffee with the girls

THE NEXT DAY, after a night of quietly seething with Jean unaware, Stacey met the girls at a local café to savor a cup of coffee and a bit of gossip. The "girls" were in fact ladies, other mothers that Stacey had met while dropping kids off at school, picking them up, taking them to piano lessons or tennis. And chaperoning school field trips. You learned a lot about a person by how they handled the kid throwing up in the back of the bus, because there always was one.

These were good women. Stacey knew she could

depend on them for support. Perhaps she should confide in them? Before she could, though, Christine burst out with the latest gossip.

"Did you hear about Sophie?" she asked. The others shook their head no, Stacey included. Christine leaned in closer and lowered her voice, "Sophie found out that Marc is cheating on her. Evidently he's been boinking that young assistant of his." She took a sip of her coffee, watching their reactions over the brim of her mug. There were various reactions of disbelief and a general "*non!*" from the group.

"*Oui!*" she continued, setting down the mug. "She followed them to a hotel. When they came out and they started to drive away in separate cars, Sophie rammed the mistress's car." There were chuckles and more shaking of heads. "The paramedics came. The police came. The mistress has whiplash, but Marc convinced her not to press charges." Having dropped her bomb, Christine leaned back, raising her mug again to her lips. This was a signal to the others to comment.

And they did.

It was surprising that five women who were such good friends could have such different opinions. Or, rather, four, because Stacey was careful to make the appropriate listening noises, the mmm-hmmms, the nods, and the occasional shaking of her head, without actually using any words. Stacey was no longer sure she wanted to confide in her friends. She knew if she said one word, the whole truth would come tumbling out, and she didn't know yet if that was what she wanted.

So she listened: To Evelyne, whose first concern was that Sophie's insurance premiums were sure to go up now. To Isabelle, who understood the need for revenge, but violence? There's a limit. To Christine, the one who had brought up the subject in the first place, who had very strong views about airing one's dirty laundry in public. After such an embarrassing display, she couldn't possibly invite the couple to dinner any more.

"That's true," Evelyne said.

"Absolutely," Isabelle agreed. "Once they know that we know that Marc has been cheating, that makes small talk over cocktails really uncomfortable."

Patricia, who used to be a contract attorney, a career which definitely left its mark on her vision of romantic life, had a different take on all this.

"A marriage is a contract just like any other," she said. "There are two parties, the husband and the wife. Generally, the wife takes care of the household, either doing all the housework and child-rearing herself or managing those who do. We put the meals on the table, clean clothes in the closets. There is a tacit agreement that we have sex and only with one another. He broke his side of the deal; Sophie should stop hers. She should stop washing his clothes, stop making his dinner, and she should definitely stop having sex with him."

There were murmurs amongst the others, some in agreement, some not.

"She wants revenge?" she continued. "Then Sophie should dedicate all the time she used to spend on making their house a home to taking care of herself. Work out, buy some new clothes, a make-over. She should look fabulous and feel fabulous, then get out there and meet someone who can appreciate her."

Stacey was shocked. Four different reactions to the affair and not a single one accepted it. She spoke, carefully, trying to keep the tone of her voice even, disinterested.

"But I thought you French were more open about that sort of thing. That you accepted affairs as par for the course."

The ladies laughed.

"All these years, and you're still so American!" Evelyne said.

"No way," Isabelle added. Stacey looked puzzled.

"That was our mothers," Patricia explained. "Grand-mothers, even. Our generation expects more."

"Thank God times have changed," Christine said, before leading the conversation back to Sophie.

The ladies went on to talk about other examples they had known. Or heard of. After an hour, when the conversation petered out and the last drops of coffee were long gone, they all went back to their separate lives and concerns.

For Stacey, however, the discussions about the *malheurs de Sophie* made her own predicament even more complicated. Complicated? Or nuanced? Or was it the same thing? The French loved complicated analyses, which explained the importance of philosophy and politics. They trained high school students to debate, constructing arguments, point, counterpoint. A verbal joust. It didn't matter who won, as long as the argument was well constructed.

As Evelyne had said, Stacey was still so American: pragmatic, no patience for all the philosophizing, wanting results. They all condemned Sophie's reactions but Stacey understood. She chuckled to herself. Sophie certainly got results.

7

Snooping

A S SOON AS STACEY got home, she made herself a sandwich, grabbed a diet coke and sat down to think. She was not going to take Jean's infidelity lying down.

From time immemorial, women discovered their men were cheating from a dab of lipstick on his collar or a strand of long hair on his suit jacket. Stacey had learned from an email. Times changed.

Back in the day, after seeing the lipstick, the wife rummaged through the husband's pockets and especially his wallet, looking for clues. *We've all seen this in the movies*, Stacey thought. These methods were still valid. What was it called? Material evidence? Now spouses could take it further. Much further.

His phone.

If she knew his security code, or if he didn't have that damn finger-print recognition thing, she could go in and look at his address book, his text messages, his list of outgoing and incoming calls. Of course, that would suppose that he left his phone lying around. He didn't. It was like his third hand or second brain. He even took it to the bathroom. He didn't actually take it in the shower; it wasn't waterproof. Could there be an opportunity...? She had read that the mobile phone was a boon to extra-marital affairs. Blackberry was called the adulterer's phone of choice since compromising text messages didn't appear on the screen upon arrival, thus affording greater discretion over the iPhone. She chuckled. Jean must not have done his research.

Smart phones also allowed their users to go onto dating sites without leaving traces in the browser of the family computer. So convenient. You could pretend you were checking emails but actually be reading messages for hook-ups with potential lovers. Stacey had laughed at a recent scandal. One of those web sites, known to be used by married people, had been hacked. The hackers had "outed" the members, exposing their affairs to the world. At the time, she had laughed at them getting their just desserts. Now, she had a thought for the families and the shock of learning in such a public way of the betrayal of the spouse or parent. Imagine learning your dad was cheating on your mom when you saw his name in the newspapers.

"Don't complicate things," Stacey told herself. The phone presented too many difficulties but what about his car? She bet he left things lying around in the car.

If she could find an excuse to get some "alone time" with his car, she could look through the trunk, the glove compartment, and other nooks and crannies for clues, or 'intel' as the TV series called it. She could also look at his GPS. From that, she could probably work out where the skank lived, where they met each other, where they ... well, she didn't need to spell it all out, did she.

Looking through his car and looking through the GPS would mean waiting until Jean came home from work—and Stacey couldn't bear to wait that long. Microwaves, video on demand and Amazon same-day delivery had created a collective impatience, a desire for instant gratification, and Stacey was just like everyone else. She wanted information and she wanted it now.

What about internet? She wouldn't have to wait to

try that.

She sat down in front of the computer, cracked her fingers in the time-honored safecracker's gesture, flipped the switch, typed in her password and went to work. Having her name already made it child's play. *If you're going to have an affair with a married man*, Stacey thought, *you shouldn't use your real name for your email address.* From that brief glimpse at Jean's emails, she knew his mistress's first and last names.

Berenice.

Jaunatre.

Free.fr

Paris region

There were two. She clicked on the Facebook profile of this one. Thirteen years old. "Jean is a philanderer, not a pedophile," Stacey murmured to herself. No Facebook for the other person. Hmmm. LinkedIn? That was disappointing, no photo. Very brief history, just "free-lance writer," *Montreuil*, a degree in journalism from the *Ecole Supérieur de Journalisme* à Paris. The age surprised Stacey; Berenice was only three years younger than she was.

She typed the date and name of the journalism school into the search bar, added "graduates," and lo and behold found a blog of a classmate with photos from a reunion, the kind of thing people create to share photos in the afterglow of an event and then forget about, as they move on to the next thing. Thank God people were careless! She quickly clicked through the photos, reading captions. Ah, there she was. The caption clearly didn't give the names in left to right order or Michelle had a glandular problem, but it did mean that Berenice was one of the three women in the photo. Weeding through more photos and more captions, Stacey located four photos with the name in the captions, placed them side by side and found only one common denominator.

It was her!

It was her?

Really, Jean was cheating on Stacey with *her*?

She looked at the photos and saw a woman who was about her age. Medium height. Dirty blond hair cut and styled to show that she was trying. A little make-up. Gold hoops in her ears, a little crass. Her clothes were pretty good. Not high end but not cheap, the style suited both her figure and the event. She looked happy to see her former classmates and was at ease in the group.

She was a little younger, a little shorter, a little more stylish than Stacey, and not at all what Stacey had been expecting. One imagines a homewrecker to look more like Raquel Welch or Jessica Rabbit, not just an incremental improvement on oneself.

She chose the photo that was a close-up and printed it out. "Now, the address."

LinkedIn had given a city name. Stacey entered it into the white pages, along with Berenice's name, and *voilà*, the address and phone number appeared. She printed that out, too.

Name, address and photo—that's a good start, but it doesn't tell me who she really is, thought Stacey. Did she really want to know more about Berenice? Or was it some sort of compulsion, like when you eat one M&M, then another, and suddenly the whole bag was gone?

Stacey went back to Google, this time typing both the name and the city. Sorting through the answers one by one, winding her way through a virtual maze, the trail taking her sometimes closer, sometimes further away from her quarry. Little by little, she reconstructed parts of the story.

Stacey did a search on Berenice's name, then clicked on "images." Among the results, she spotted a photo of her husband and Berenice, both on skis, arm in arm in front of a beautiful mountain panorama. She double-clicked on that photo to arrive at the website for a photographer at a ski resort, one of those who stalked children and grandparents at the bottom of the ski slopes to guilt-trip them into extra sales. The photo of Berenice and Jean was next to a photo of her husband alone, amidst the mountain tops. Stacey knew that photo! February last year, Jean had said he was going skiing with Olivier, he needed to get away, wanted to do something athletic.

Athletic, my eye. Sure, sex gets the heart rate up, but athletic?

She remembered when he came home from the trip. He had been so tired. He had complained how Olivier skied too fast, went on all the black slopes, never let him recuperate. She remembered how she had comforted him, had drawn him a hot bath, put in those special bath salts for sore muscles. He had purred like a cat.

What a sucker she had been!

She pulled herself out of her *reverie* and went back to the Google results. A few minutes later, on the Facebook page of one of Berenice's friends, she found a photo entitled "Berenice Jaunatre in Rome with 'he who must not be named'." April, year before last. They smiled at her from the Spanish Steps, squinting against the bright Italian sun, looking very happy.

Rome! She had always wanted to go to Rome. When she had learned his company was sending him to a conference there, she had suggested that she go along. It would be a fun escapade. He had said no. There would be breakfast meetings before the conference and evening team-building events after, he had said. Every day. She just didn't realize how stressful and intense these conferences could be. Besides, who would look after the kids? Always understanding, she didn't push the point. Now, of course, she understood. Only too well.

She ran upstairs to get the calendar from two years before, the one she had saved because she loved the photos. She flipped through the pages, found April, where she had marked Jean's departure and return dates. Back to the computer, she searched the name of the conference and year. Ah, blessed internet where nothing ever fades away. In the world of teenage bullying via social media, the longevity of computer files was a problem. Today, for her, it was a good thing. She clicked on the conference program schedule, compared the dates to her calendar. He had been away for five days. Turns out it was a three-day event. The photo had been posted on Facebook the first day of the conference. *She* had been there the whole time and evidently had bragged about the trip to her friends.

The more she found out about Jean's lover, the more she pieced together their story, the angrier she got. Really angry. It was as if they had disturbed a primal force in her, awakening the she-wolf inside who had been slumbering but now sprang to action to protect her den. This feeling was big, powerful, dangerous, and was surprising to someone as mild-mannered as Stacey. It was reminiscent of the scene in *Raiders of the Lost Ark*, when the Nazis opened the Ark of the Covenant, releasing a destructive force which flew everywhere at once, killing them all in horrific, painful deaths.

That was Stacey.

Inside the baby blue twin set raged a fiery beast who would stop at nothing to protect her tribe from the invader, in this case, Berenice Jaunatre of *Montreuil*.

As Stacey walked by the bookcase where the DVDs were stored, *Fatal Attraction* caught her eye, the classic film about a cheating husband who regrets his indiscretion. She took it out, turning it over and over in her hands, looking at the photos on the jacket, remembering scenes from the movie, particularly the famous final scene in the bathtub. Before thinking it through and for reasons she couldn't fully explain, she moved to the kitchen table where she wrapped it up in plain brown kraft paper, which would give no clues as to the sender. She found the computer print-outs with Berenice's address and carefully copied it onto the package, all in capital letters so her handwriting couldn't be traced. At least, that's what the detective novels said.

She added some stamps, then walked down the street to the nearest mailbox, a yellow metal one on the train station wall. Almost in a daze, she examined her package once again and put it in the mailbox slot, hesitating a fraction of a second before watching the DVD slide all the way in.

She smiled to herself, satisfied. That felt strangely good.

For the next few days, Stacey caught herself smiling, imagining Berenice's reaction. Was the message behind the DVD clear enough? Maybe it was too subtle? Maybe she didn't know the movie. It dated back to 1987. Stacey shook her head, shaking off her worries at the same time. If she didn't know the movie already, she would watch it, wanting to know why someone had sent it to her. She would be alone, at night, and would get to the bathtub scene. Stacey laughed again. Either way it played out, it played well for Stacey.

8

The DVD

THE DAY THE DVD should have arrived, Stacey and Jean were having dinner, just the two of them. Laura had gone to her musician boyfriend's gig and David to a geek-a-thon with his buddies. Stacey watched Jean closely. No real difference, perhaps slightly more tense than usual. Was that a tic below his left eye? No. She felt deflated.

What was I expecting? she chided herself. If he could sleep with her for three years without me seeing the signs, why would I expect to see something now?

Then, Jean's mobile phone rang in his pocket. He took it out, looked at the caller ID, frowned, pressed reject, put it away and picked up his knife and fork again. The phone rang again. He put the silverware down, almost banging them on the table, before standing up and taking his phone out again.

"Yes," he answered, leaving the room. He headed toward his study, listening to whatever the caller was saying, closing the door behind him before saying "I told you never to call me at home." If Stacey had had any doubts, she knew now who was calling.

She got up silently, tiptoed to the door and listened. A one-sided conversation, but instructive all the same. "I didn't send you anything.... Arrived today? No note?" he made a noise like someone was strangling him. More silence. "It must have been someone else" Pause. "Honestly, she wouldn't have the nerve to do something like that." Stacey stifled a chuckle.

Another pause, then "Just not possible. She's good with the house and kids, but I just don't think she's capable of..."

On the other side of the door, Stacey fumed. What? Not daring? Not capable of anything outside of housework? How little Jean knew her! She was a complete person, multi-dimensional, not some flat stereotype.

The conversation behind the door marked another pause and a change in tone. Coldly. "I don't know who else you're seeing. I bet there are plenty of wives who could have sent it." More silence, interrupted by a word here or there. Clearly she was angry and he couldn't get a word in, so he changed tactics. "Berenice," he practically cooed, "you know that's not what I was saying. I would never think that about you."

I would, thought Stacey.

"OK, OK. I'm sorry. I didn't mean that." Silence. A sigh. "OK. You're right."

As she listened to the one-sided end of an argument and, more disturbingly, to the one-sided making up, Stacey accidently bumped the chair just outside the study door.

"Listen, I'd better go," Jean started to say. She tiptoed quickly back to the kitchen table, putting some of the food on her plate back into the serving dish to make it look like she had continued eating while waiting for him. Jean, visibly shaken, came back to the table with a huff.

"Something wrong, dear?" Stacey asked sweetly, despite feeling hurt by what she had overheard.

"The office," he grumbled. "We've got a new intern who makes mistake after mistake. Creates more work for the rest of us. Sometimes, I don't know why we even hire them."

"You work so hard already," she added, *faux* admiringly. His ego appeased, Jean's bad mood passed, making him surprisingly good company as they finished their meal. He told witty stories about his colleagues at work, a few vignettes about a big client. Jean could be very funny when he wanted to. And charming. She had forgotten how charming he could be. She refilled their wine glasses with the end of the bottle they'd been drinking.

He went and got another red from the cellar, which they polished off as well over the course of the evening, regaling her with "the Office Chronicles," raising his storytelling to an art form. She wasn't sure that all these stories were true, nor that they had all happened to him, but it didn't matter. They made for a good tale, and that was the point. She was having a good evening, basking in his attention and charm. It felt like when they were dating and he wasn't yet sure of her, did not yet take her for granted.

It was a good evening.

She loved him.

Which made the knowledge of his cheating all the more painful.

They were still at the table, talking, laughing, and sipping their wine when the kids arrived home. They both looked as surprised to see their parents as the parents were to realize they had spent four hours together, simply enjoying one another's company.

It had been a long time.

9

Stalking

THE RESEARCH SHE HAD done online all seemed a little incomplete. What she needed, Stacey felt, was to meet the trollop in person. No, not actually meet her, but see her, in the flesh, study her in her natural habitat and try to understand what Jean saw in her. She wanted to observe Berenice at close quarters, almost like Jane Goodall in the jungles of Africa.

She would have to be careful, though; there was a risk that Berenice would recognize her. Stacey had no idea if

Jean had talked about her. He had a photo of the two of them in his wallet. Berenice had surely seen that, but it was so old and she had changed so much over the years that she didn't think she was recognizable. Possibly Berenice had looked her up on the web, just as Stacey had done, and so had seen more recent photos. That was more likely. She would take her precautions.

Stacey glanced at her watch. If she hurried, she could probably catch Berenice on her lunch break. She grabbed her handbag and started out the door, then caught herself and went back to get a big floppy hat, a scarf and dark glasses. Just in case.

Stacey arrived in front of the office building where Berenice worked, feeling a combination of excitement and fear which made her stomach churn, something a moth must feel as it's drawn inexorably toward the light. She was just in time to see her leave the building and head down the sidewalk. Stacey followed in her car, hoping against all hopes to find a parking spot. Berenice turned left at the first intersection; Stacey got stuck at a red light. As soon as it turned green, she turned left too, catching up to Berenice only to see her head up a stairway. Damn! She was going to lose her. If she didn't have the car... Stacey's thoughts trailed on, plotting out what would make her more successful in the future.

The near future, to be exact, because the next day she was there, in front of the office building, a full thirty minutes before the time Berenice had gone to lunch the previous day. Stacey had taken the train in order to avoid any traffic or parking delays. She had dressed in business attire, granted a little out of fashion since it had been several years since she had last worked, but still close enough to make her nondescript in the business district. She found a bench from where she had a view of the building's entrance, sat down, and opened a newspaper, surveilling the comings and goings over the top of her paper like a spy in a Hollywood movie.

Like her clothes, her methods were a little outdated since everyone around her had his eyes glued on the screen of his mobile phone; no one else had a paper. No matter, though, since no one paid any attention to her, let alone notice her surveilling the building.

After forty-five minutes, by which time Stacey had actually read the newspaper from cover to cover, Berenice exited the building accompanied by another woman. The two chatted amicably as they walked down the street and turned left, just as Berenice had done the day before, passing Stacey's bench on the way, not even glancing in her direction. Letting out a sigh of relief, Stacey waited a minute or two as the ladies put a little distance between them, then got up, folded her newspaper and started off in pursuit.

Tailing them was easy. Stacey had read enough Raymond Chandler and had seen enough detective shows on TV to know the proper techniques. Well, maybe not 'proper technique' but good enough. She followed the duo up the stairs, across a public square and into a shopping mall. Stacey followed them from store to store then, when they sat down to eat a salad in the food court, was lucky enough to find a table next to theirs, screened from their view by a trellis and potted plants so she could eavesdrop safely. Berenice and her friend must have been colleagues, given that they talked first about work and then about a difficult colleague before discussing their plans for the weekend. Nothing about Jean. Berenice was discreet; Stacey, disappointed. *What did I expect?* she asked herself. She did learn a few details about Berenice's daily life, her likes and dislikes, and so was starting to form a better idea of who she was.

The two ladies got up to leave. Stacey stayed in her seat, preferring to give up her surveillance for the time being.

10

Revenge

I T TURNED OUT that knowing who Berenice was did nothing to dissipate Stacey's anger. *Au contraire.* Seeing her in person had caused something to shift inside of Stacey. A seed had been planted when her girlfriends discussed Sophie's car crash of a marriage, then Stacey had a small taste of it with the DVD...

How do women get revenge after being cheated on? With dignity, as Patricia suggested? With discretion, as Christine preferred? As always, Stacey felt the answer was on the internet, so she sat down in front of Google and typed, "revenge on husband's mistress," "revenge on cheating husband," and the same in French. She read the results, one by one, plunging deeper and deeper into the sick, sad world of public shaming, where women created google-searchable blogs to "get back at that bitch," left the mistresses' names and phone numbers on porn sites, created fake Facebook pages to post the lovers' sexy text messages and then "friend" everyone who was friends with the mistress on her real Facebook account. Social media becoming antisocial media. One woman went so far as to purchase a billboard to display her husband's and his mistress' license plate numbers so commuters on the LA highway could "honk if you see the cheaters."

It was brutal.

There were many examples of destroying the man's belongings. Cars had "cheater" "adulterer" and "scumbag" written on them in nail polish or with a car key. "High class prostitute, 800€ for the night" was written on the passenger door of the woman's car. Garage doors were spray painted with similar messages. Another favorite was to take a scissor to the husband's shirts or suits. One woman did better. She sold her man's clothes on eBay, modeling shirts wearing only the shirt and a thong, and modeling his favorite shorts wearing nothing else. *Look at that body! How could he cheat on that?* Stacey thought. Then, as an afterthought, *I bet she made a bundle.*

Her mind buzzed with ideas, the good, bad, and ugly, and she needed to let them settle.

She took out a blank sheet of paper, pencil at hand. *The pencil is important, not a pen*, she thought. In French schools, they taught the children to write with a pen as early as kindergarten, and with a fountain pen starting in first grade. It was too young. After years of coaching her children in the fine art of cursive writing with a fountain pen, small fingers fumbling to hold the pen at the proper angle, to refill the cartridge at the right time, to avoid the telltale splotches that would anger the teacher, her tablecloths could attest that first grade, even fourth grade, was just too young. Ink was messy; it was also definitive. How could you have definitive ideas when you were six years old?

True to her American upbringing, she preferred a pencil, ideally soft lead, with a good pink eraser at the end. A pencil didn't splot. A pencil let you change your mind, evolve in your ideas. As you put your ideas to paper, as they developed in black and white, you could better see the gaps in logic, the missing steps. With a pencil, you could erase and start over, choose a more precise word, take out that dangling modifier or sentence fragment.

Revenge, she thought, *should be treated as any other project; for it to come out right, you need to plan.* She was an excellent planner. All those meals, with starter, main course, and dessert, all the complicated recipes with variable cooking and prep times. They didn't just happen. You had to retro plan.

If you invited eight people for a dinner party, what did you need to know? Any diabetics? Gluten intolerances? Other medical concerns? What time of year was it? If it was autumn, maybe choose a roast with some sort of mushroom. What about *lapin chasseur*? Yum. Pumpkins and winter squash came in at that time of year, so what about that roasted pumpkin and pine nut salad as a starter? For dessert, apple tart would be nice, again a seasonal fruit. Julia Child had a wonderful recipe.

What took longest to cook? The limiting factor was going to be the oven, since the apple compote in the tart, the tart itself and the pumpkin all required the oven, which made hunter-style rabbit, a stove-top dish, a good choice. The tart pastry needed 30 to 60 minutes to rest between when she stirred it up and when she rolled it out, which indicated the prep time frame:

Measure out the flour, mix in the other dry ingredients, cut in small chunks of cold butter, add just the minimum amount of water to bind, then chill in fridge for at least ½ hour.

Cut apples for tart filling, roast in oven.

Cut pumpkin into bite-sized pieces, add the spices and toss to coat evenly. When apples were done, take out to cool and put pumpkin in to roast.

Roll out pastry, put into tart pan. Take pumpkin out of the oven, put in tart. Reduce heat.

While the pie shell baked, chop the onions and prepare the mushrooms for the *lapin chasseur*. Sear the meat in a mixture of oil and butter, remove from the pan, then sauté the onion five minutes. Add bouillon, white wine and tomato paste. Bring to a boil.

Which gave you just enough time to mash the cooked apple mixture, then, when the pie crust was golden brown, fill it with the apple compote. Peel and cut apple slices, place onto compote in a spiral pattern. Bake for another 25 – 30 minutes.

Back to the *lapin chasseur*, add the rabbit pieces back to the pan and let simmer for over an hour in the bouillon – white wine broth. During this time, sauté the mushrooms in butter, add lemon juice, salt and pepper, then set aside to add to the rabbit at the last minute. Finish plating the roasted pumpkin on a bed of salad greens with pine nuts and slivered parmesan. Give it a last drizzle of olive oil.

Set and decorate the table.

Change clothes, touch up make-up.

Set out nibbles to accompany the *aperitifs*, the pre-dinner cocktails.

Oh! The *aperitifs*! She saw in the plan that she forgot to set a time aside for chilling the champagne. Her plan didn't include pre-heating the oven, either. A cold oven would set her prep time back by 20 minutes, not leaving her the time to relax and change clothes before the guests arrived, giving a more relaxed tone of the entire evening.

This was why you plan. In writing. Then you reread, looked for omissions, time conflicts. When you executed the plan, you could more easily adapt to unforeseen circumstances (a soufflé that gives its dying breath, a guest who arrives early, a husband who arrives late) because the rest was under control.

This was exactly what she needed to do for her revenge. Like a meal, there were three parts: create discord between the two of them, preferably irreparably, hurt the floozy, and get even with her husband. Were there examples to follow, like Julia Child's recipe? A flurry of ideas flew from her pencil, quickly covering the page in gray.

With a critical eye, she reread what she had written. Like the oven, were there limiting factors? She jotted a few notes on her paper. Was there a need for time for things to simmer, like the *lapin chasseur*? Again, she wrote down a few more items. Was there an order to respect, like starter, main course, dessert? She numbered certain items on her page, circling some, crossing out others. A plan was starting to emerge.

Sort of.

If it were a true plan, there would be a clear goal, a "desired outcome" as they said in business. She didn't know why she was doing this, didn't know what she wanted to gain. Like a small child, she was lashing out, her anger taking the upper hand to reason, despite all the planning.

Step 1 of her plan: control the lines of communications.

A quick trip to the phone store, and Stacey was the proud owner of the Huawei Honor 5x, a phone which could take two SIM cards. As soon as the young salesman touted the conveniences of having business and personal lines on a single phone, Stacey knew it was for her. A new phone, her old SIM card and a second one kindly installed by the salesman, and she was good.

Back at home, she sat down at her computer, turned it on and practically danced with anticipation as she waited for it to boot up. For once, she found the process to be interminably long. Interminably. That was a good word.

Terminal, end. In, the negative, no end. Endless. Five syllables, which made it a long word, two syllables longer than endlessly, those two extra syllables better making the point. Onomatopoeia meant a word that sounded like the thing it described, that phonetically imitated its objects, like the buzz of a bee or the tick tock of a clock. So what would you call a word that structurally imitated its object?

The computer beep drew her out of her musings. She went straight to Yahoo. She created a new account, dupont.jean@yahoo.fr, then another email address, jeandupont@yahoo.fr. All the security questions... she knew what he would answer. After twenty-five years of marriage, she knew all the answers.

Revise that. If she really did know all the answers, she wouldn't be spending her afternoon creating fictitious email accounts to get revenge on her husband's bit on the side.

Stacey pushed that thought aside and logged into one of the accounts, clicked on "create new email," then typed in Berenice's address. Subject line? Hmmm. "New email address"

"Dear Berenice,

I've just realized that Stacey has hacked my email account, so I have created this new one. I don't know how much she knows, but I wanted to warn you not to trust anything coming from that account. I have a new phone, too. The number is ..."

Stacey paused, a pleased grin appearing on her face. Damn, that was good. She continued to type.

"I love you. I want to hold you, but first I must keep us safe from Stacey.

- Jean"

Ha! That should do it. If Berenice didn't get the message from *Fatal Attraction* that wives could be dangerous, she'll get it now.

Jean's turn now.

"*Chéri*," she wrote from the second Jean Dupont address. "Someone has hacked my email account. I know how much discretion means to you so I made this new account. You notice the address? Think of me as your lustful evil twin. Ha ha. I have a new phone, too, just to be doubly careful. The number is ...

"*Je t'aime*,

Berenice."

She could just see Jean congratulating himself for having chosen a minx who was so careful, so protective of his reputation.

She barely had time to log out of the email accounts before the phone beeped. A text message from Berenice. Stacey replied, imitating Jean's style, Berenice wrote back immediately... and Stacey found herself sucked into the weird predicament of writing love letters (love emails?) to her husband's strumpet. Stacey wrote what she would have wanted to hear from Jean, the way he used to talk to her. A twisted Cyrano de Bergerac, motivated by anger instead of love. Given the response, either she was a much better writer than Jean, or Berenice wasn't the brightest light bulb in the chandelier.

Berenice was clearly always on the look-out for a message from Jean. Jean, however, was much slower to respond, much more measured in his replies, just as she had expected. At the end of the day, probably after his last appointment and before driving home, he sent a text message, "I got a new phone number, too. J" Stacey was surprised—or was it hurt she was feeling?-- but quickly sent back something, trying to sound sexy, younger and eager, all in the abbreviated style of a text.

Step 2: make use of all that internet research

One of the best stories Stacey had read was about a woman in the U.S. who learned that her husband was cheating on her. She gave him an ultimatum; he chose the other woman (or women, the web site didn't say) and so they divorced. The problem for the soon-to-be-ex-wife was that she loved her home but couldn't afford to purchase his half at current market prices. What to do? She couldn't change the amount of money the banks were willing to lend her. Could she somehow influence the house's market value? She went to the supermarket and bought ten pounds of shrimp, which she then put inside all the curtain rods in the house. After a few days, there was an odd smell throughout the house, which put off potential buyers and real-estate agents alike. After two weeks, then a month, the smell grew stronger and stronger, as did the husband's desperation to sell, so the couple decided to lower the price. Again and again, until the asking price was low enough that the wife could afford it and she purchased the house. She kindly packed all the husband's things for the movers, including the curtain rods for use in his new house.

Urban legend? Reality? It didn't really matter, since the story made Stacey realize that a DIY rotting-food stink bomb was doable. She could even include several food groups.

And so she did. Diced potatoes in water hidden in an open container under the driver's seat of Jean's car. It was only a matter of time before the stench ruined his sweet ride. For Berenice, chicken in milk, skillfully hidden in the base of a potted plant which Stacey left on her doorstep. Berenice would be delighted by the gift and, once the chicken went bad, search for the source of the smell.

Stacey was aflame with ideas, sometimes leaving a trace of lipstick on Jean's collar or spraying a woman's perfume for Berenice to find, sometimes delaying their text messages until it was too late for the *rendezvous* to happen, sometimes changing Berenice's messages just enough for Jean to wonder if it was really meant for him.

A lunch date between the two lovers? No problem. She transferred their messages back and forth then, the morning before their date, as Jean showered, Stacey took his wallet and carefully removed the credit cards and all but ten Euros. She opened his dresser drawer and laid them inside, where he sometimes put his wallet when he didn't need to carry it. She closed the drawer seconds before he stepped from the bathroom to the bedroom to get dressed.

It was a cinch. Either Berenice would have to foot the bill, and Stacey was sure she wouldn't be "in the mood" after that, or the restaurant owner would call the cops. Either way, a win for Stacey.

11

Opéra

A DAY LATER, SHE intercepted another email. Clearly, Jean was trying to make amends for the bad luck they were having with their assignations.

"*Chérie,*" he wrote in an email. "I was able to get tickets to *Carmen* for tomorrow. I know how much you love it. They were sold out, but I was able to call in a few favors. The tickets are attached to this email. I'll need to come straight from the office, so print out your ticket and I'll meet you there. *Je t'embrasse*, Jean."

Stacey couldn't believe her luck. The tickets were attached? Wasn't that handy! She didn't even need to scheme this time. *The plan fell right into my lap*, she thought as she re-routed the email to Berenice, attachments and all.

The next evening, Stacey arrived early, to make sure her print-outs of the tickets were used before Jean and Berenice could use theirs. She waited on the stairway in the Opéra Bastille, leaning over the balustrade to observe the foyer below.

Part of the opera experience is to see and be seen, so no one thought twice if they even noticed her people-watching those below, nor did they wonder why she stayed there, immobile, for such a long time. Perhaps fifteen minutes after she started her guard duty, Stacey saw Jean and Berenice arrive at the ticket control point at the bottom of the staircase. Berenice handed her print-out to Jean, who then extended both his ticket and hers to the young woman with the scanner.

The young woman read the code bar on the first ticket; her machine made a strange noise so she scanned the code bar again. The machine made the same noise. The young woman peered at a small screen on the device, frowned, then tried the second ticket, with the same result.

She tried both tickets again. The line of people

waiting to enter started backing up. The people next in line started grumbling, showing their impatience.

"I'm sorry sir," the young woman said to Jean. "There seems to be some sort of a problem. The scanner says that these tickets have already been used."

"That's impossible!" Jean replied. The young woman politely held her ground, Jean repeated his position, the queue backed up even more. A bell rang, indicating that the opera was about to start.

The tone of the discussion got uglier, until the young woman made a gesture to a colleague, who said something into his shirt sleeve. At Jean's side appeared two large men, two George Foremans in suits and ties.

"Sir," said one of them, taking Jean's arm, "you'll need to come with us." Jean protested, as the second man took Berenice by the elbow. The duo escorted the pair of lovers down the hallway, through a discrete door in the wall. Stacey could hear Jean protesting the whole way, above the din of the other concert-goers. She felt pleased with herself, a little proud, even. She had been spontaneous. She had seized an opportunity and it was working out perfectly.

The bell rang a second time. Stacey turned away from the balustrade and made her way to her seat. Orchestra seats, center section. Jean had to have really powerful connections to get seats this good. As she sat down, the young man in the adjoining seat turned toward her with a large smile and handed her a program. Alain, her friend Evelyne's son.

Stacey had known Alain since he was a boy. As a small child, he had loved "Peter and the Wolf" and "The Magic Flute." As a teenager, his taste had progressed to Vivaldi's Four Seasons and Beethoven's 5th, and then Händel's Messiah, before hitting his twenties and developing a taste for an even larger repertoire.

Unfortunately for Alain, the meager salary of a first job combined with the high Parisian rents meant he could rarely afford live concerts, let alone opera. For Alain, tonight was the ultimate luxury: Opéra Bastille, world-class celebrity singers, two of the best seats in the house. His excitement was palpable.

That excitement was exactly why Stacey had chosen to share this moment with him.

There was a certain justice to it. Jean who had lied, cheated and betrayed, was punished. Alain, who worked so hard but could not afford the thing he loved most, was rewarded. Wasn't that how life is supposed to work?

The conductor took his place. The audience applauded. The orchestra started to play. As the curtain rose, Stacey relaxed into the velour cushion, pleased to have created havoc for Jean and Berenice and to have seen the results of her plotting for the first time!

To have created havoc, to have seen the results first-hand and to have given such happiness to the young man seated next to her. It was a wonderful evening.

12

Restaurant mayhem

DESPITE ALL THE MAYHEM Stacey was causing, despite all the recent failures, Jean kept trying. He proposed another restaurant, La Trattoria, the next day at 12:30, then "We'll stop by Christophe's afterward."

Christophe was Jean's childhood friend. A hardened bachelor, he had never shown any interest in Jean's wife or children. Stacey and Christophe got along, mainly because they had to, but had never gotten to the point where they enjoyed one another's company. Christophe wouldn't be there; he was currently living in London for four months. Jean must be using his place for his romantic trysts.

Stacey re-read Jean's text.

Quel goujat! *What a jerk!* she thought. *That's hardly a romantic invitation. We can do better than that.* She took out her mobile phone and started typing "*Mi amore.* Remember our wonderful moments together in Rome? Let's eat and drink in memory of the City of Love. Meet me at La Trattoria, tomorrow at 1. Wear that sexy dress you had in Rome. Drives me wild. Longingly, J."

Ha! That should do it.

Berenice texted back almost immediately. Their *rendezvous* was confirmed. *Interesting word, 'rendezvous,'* thought Stacey. In French, its language of origin, it meant 'appointment.' Any appointment, including the dog groomer, the dentist, pretty much anything. If you wanted to refer to Jean and Berenice's tryst, you would say "*rendezvous galant.*" In English, rendezvous meant the illicit meeting of two lovers, which just showed what the English thought of the French.

The next day, the kids went off to school, as usual. Jean got ready for work, also as usual, as if it were just a normal day. Stacey was surprised to see no sign, nothing unusual, nothing whatsoever to indicate that his day would be anything out of the ordinary.

"Big day?" she asked, as he finished knotting his tie.

"No, not really." He looked in the mirror and tugged his tie a little to the left. "You know, department meeting to start, then a couple of appointments with clients."

"But you look so nice. Like you want to impress someone."

Jean smiled and gave her a quick kiss.

"I'm glad you think so, but no, just those meetings. Oh—I do need to finish the strategy report for ..." and he trailed off in a detailed explanation about a difficult client.

Around 11, she left for La Trattoria, to scope out the neighborhood and find a good spot from which to spy. She rarely went to the part of Paris where Jean's office was located. It was far from the house and didn't have a lot in the way of shopping. It did, however, have a lot of restaurants, mid to high end, catering to lunch-time office workers and after-work drinkers. La Trattoria looked nicer than most. Jean knew how to dine well, she gave him that.

She was in luck. La Trattoria was on a pedestrian street and, like the surrounding restaurants, had tables on the front terrace. The weather was nice so Jean would surely choose a table there. She looked around and saw a place across the way.

Again, luck was with her, or maybe the early hour, since most Parisians don't go to lunch until 1 pm or later. She found a table in front of the window, placed at an angle, so that the big ficus in the corner screened her from view yet allowed her to see the restaurant terrace with perfection. The waiter brought the menu, along with a blackboard covered in the day's specials. She had forty-five minutes ahead of her, so she took her time ordering, despite the waiter coming back every few minutes, asking if she was ready to order. *There is a fine line,* she thought, *between being attentive and being a pest.*

She carefully studied the list of starters and main courses and chose those with the longest cooking times but could not be prepared in advance. No stews, no pot-au-feu which would be simmering for hours and would only require being plated. Her choices were off the *prix fixe* menu, which meant a higher bill at the end. Usually, she was more careful with money but, what the hell? With everything Jean must be spending on that bitch. Stacey, could treat herself, too. The waiter started warming up to her.

"I see that Madame is a *connoisseur*. May I suggest a wine to go with that?"

"You certainly may. Perhaps a different one with each course?"

The waiter's smile grew even wider.

He came back, set an empty wine glass in front of her, then ceremoniously uncorked a bottle of Côteaux de Peyriac blanc, smelled the cork on the end of the corkscrew, poured a small amount into the glass and said "If Madame would like to taste."

Madame did want to taste. Stacey held the glass up to study the color, then brought it closer to her nose, smelled, then took a small sip of wine, swishing the liquid around in her mouth as she imitated what she had seen in movies.

"Very good," she said, setting the glass down. The waiter filled it completely, then left.

About the time her first course arrived, so did Jean. He looked around, seemed a little surprised to be the first one there, then chose a table on the terrace, in full view from her vantage point behind the potted plant. She couldn't have chosen better herself. She slowly ate her *soufflé au crabe*, as slowly as she dared, while watching Jean study the menu, glance at his watch, look at the menu again, pull out his mobile phone to see if he had any messages, glance at his watch again, and so on and so on, clearly progressing from annoyed to angry as time passed.

Stacey's waiter cleared her empty dish and returned a few minutes later with the *tournedos rossini*, intoning the usual *bon appétit* as he placed the plate in front of her. He came back with another empty glass and another bottle of wine, a Lalande-de-Pomerol, and repeated the little ritual of uncorking, smelling, serving, waiting for Stacey to pronounce "Very nice" before giving her the full service. The first time, the ceremony was amusing. This time, it was keeping her from observing every minute detail going on (or not going on, at the specific moment) over at Jean's table.

The waiter paused, watching her watch the scene across the way, before turning to go and attend to the other clients who had since arrived.

Partway through the steak with *foie gras* and truffle, Berenice arrived. Stacey's fork stopped midair. Jean's jaw dropped. Stacey imagined the wait staff at La Trattoria dropping a plate or two. Berenice was dressed in a tight red dress. Skin-tight. It-might-have-been-painted-on tight. Even from across the street, Stacey could see every bump under the dress, ascertaining the presence of a thong, not panties, and the lack of a bra. The dress was cut low and cut high, neckline and hem respectively. For a night club, she looked fabulous, Stacey had to admit. For a lunch date in the business district, inappropriate.

Jean jumped up, taking off his suit jacket and throwing it around her shoulders before, somewhat forcibly, showing her to her seat, then looking around to see if anyone he knew had seen them. Only then did he lean over to kiss her, a platonic peck on each cheek instead of the romantic embrace usually reserved for one's lover. He sat down next to Berenice, and started talking animatedly, pointing to his watch, her dress, to his watch again. Berenice said something back, loudly, to which Jean replied, agitated.

From across the street, behind the window, Stacey couldn't hear anything of what was said but watched them like two actors in a silent movie whose actions were exaggerated to compensate for the lack of dialog. Suddenly, Berenice stood up, dramatically throwing the suit jacket down on the chair, slapped Jean and stormed away. Jean threw a few bills on the table and stormed the other way.

Stacey's waiter brought her *tarte au citron* and a glass of champagne. "I didn't order this," she said, pointing to the bubbly.

"I know," he answered, motioning to the terrace across the way and giving her a wry smile. "On the house. You deserve it."

She laughed, raising her glass to him in a mock toast.

On her way back to her car, Stacey passed by a florist shop. On a whim, she went in and ordered a dozen long stemmed red roses to be delivered, along with a note. "Forgive me,

J" When she gave the address to the florist, he looked at her knowingly. "Are you Mr. Dupont's new secretary?"

"No, just a temp."

"Should I send another bouquet to his wife, like I usually do?"

Stacey was taken aback. All those lovely bouquets Jean had sent her. It had never crossed her mind that every time Jean sent her a bouquet some other woman was receiving one, too. That was a lot of bouquets, over a lot of years... Stacey choked back tears and replied, simply, "No, not this time."

Of course. La Trattoria was close to Jean's office, so this was probably the closest florist as well. She had thought she was being smart, yet here she was, victim of her own cleverness.

She paid the bill in cash to cover her tracks and avoid the embarrassment of the florist learning who she really was.

13

Cancelled with regrets

O VER THE COURSE of the next few days, Stacey multiplied her observation forays into Berenice's life. The first day, she had dressed in business attire. The second day, a breezy, flowy thing which evoked an older artist-type. Another time, a tourist in Bermuda shorts, tennis shoes, baseball cap and pony tail. Stacey's imagination never failed. She followed Berenice to work, from work, to the dentist, to the supermarket.

She mixed it up with a little spur-of-the-moment

revenge, silly little things like unscrewing the lid of the salt and pepper shakers at the restaurant table or moving the rear view mirrors of Berenice's car.

Sometimes her ploys worked. Sometimes they didn't, like the time Stacey jammed chewing gum into the lock on Berenice's car door, only to see Berenice unlock the door with her remote.

It was all childish, Stacey knew, but it put a spring in her step to feel she was creating mayhem and confusion in their lives. Maybe not to the degree they had caused in hers, but she was new at this.

One day, though, it was different.

One day at breakfast, Jean said "I want to remind you that next weekend is the company annual retreat."

"Remind me? You would've had to have told me first," Stacey remarked matter-of-factly.

"That's the trouble with you," Jean insisted. "You've been so distracted lately; you don't even remember. You know this retreat is important for team-building. As one of the managers, it's important that I'm there to support it. You know how much I hate these things. I'd much rather spend the weekend at home with you, but it's important for my people."

"Of course, dear," replied Stacey, appearing to agree with him. "I know how important it is to bond with your staff." Secretly, though, she waited for the text message. It arrived several hours later, an invitation for Berenice to get away for the weekend, for 48 hours of cocooning to make up for all the difficult moments they'd been having recently. Stacey smiled. If only he knew who had created those difficult moments.

She forwarded the text to Berenice, who accepted less than a minute later, making Stacey think she spent her days watching her phone. Berenice thanked Jean for the invitation, accepted graciously and then asked where they were going, saying that she needed to know what clothes to bring. Stacey forwarded the message to Jean, as is. He answered a few hours later, saying she should bring her swim suit and her red dress. Both would be perfect for the spa at *Perros-Guirrec*. They would leave Friday after work and return back to Paris late Sunday.

Perros-Guirrec! Stacey was furious. She was the one who had found the spa years ago and had treated Jean to a romantic weekend of massage, mud baths, walks on the beach, and gourmet meals in the hotel restaurant. It was a beautiful place, discreetly luxurious. Instead of enjoying himself, though, Jean had spent the weekend worrying about how much it all cost. And now he was inviting his lover!

Stacey transferred the text to Berenice, fulminating

inwardly. *Perros-Guirrec* was a five hour drive from Paris.
If they left after work, they would arrive around midnight.
Hmmm. What could possibly spoil their weekend when
they were going to such a beautiful hotel? She thought for
a few minutes, then went to find her address book. The
card from the spa was still there, stuck inside the back
cover, where she had put it, with the dream of returning
one day. She called and asked for reception.

"Hello, reception."

"Hello. I'm calling for Mr. Jean Dupont. He has a
reservation for the weekend, next Friday to ..." she gave
the dates.

Keys tapped on a keyboard, a brief silence, then the
woman said "Oh yes, Jean Dupont, the Suite Pompadour,
late arrival. Room service breakfast pre-ordered for
Saturday morning. In-room duo massage for 11 am."

Stacey's blood boiled. Room service? Two-person
massage in the room? He was pulling out all stops. Making
an effort to control her voice, she simply said, "Mr. Dupont
has had an accident and broke his leg. He regrets it, but
he must cancel."

"Of course,"

Stacey smiled. She loved the good manners that went
with high end establishments. "Will it be possible to send
a confirmation of the cancellation? I'll give you his email

address so you can send it directly to him." Then added one of the bogus Jean.Dupont email addresses she had created. Within minutes she received the cancellation.

14

Ça suffit!

JEAN HAD TAKEN Berenice to Rome, the city Stacey had always dreamed of, and now he was taking her to Perros-Guirrec, the romantic getaway Stacey had taken so much trouble to find. *Ça suffit*! Enough was enough!

It was time to stop the fun and games and do something to put an end to all this.

Just as she formulated this thought, her phone beeped, a text from Berenice telling Jean how excited she was to go away with him and, to celebrate, the next day she would take off work to buy that lovely lingerie he had liked so much in the window of *Tentation Lingérie*.

Stacey did not transfer the message. Instead, she resolved to stake out the shop the next day and confront Berenice.

And so she did. The next morning she didn't look for a disguise as was her custom but chose a blouse Jean loved, with a scarf Jean had given her for her birthday and pearl earrings he had given her for their wedding anniversary. She was decked out in full regalia of the *bourgeoise*, the legitimate wife, when she left the house.

She arrived at *Tentation Lingérie* as the store opened. She could see from the street that Berenice was not inside, so she loitered on the sidewalk for almost a full hour before Berenice arrived. Berenice was quick. In the few minutes it took Stacey to enter the store, Berenice was already in the changing room, taking skimpy bits of lace from the saleslady through the closed curtain.

Stacey fled.

She would confront Berenice, but a clothed Berenice.

From the lingerie store, Stacey followed Berenice to the aesthetician's (*waxing*, Stacey thought, as she observed the redness around Berenice's eyebrows and upper lip when she came out of the store), a dress shop, a shoe store... Each time, Stacey tried, but failed, to confront her.

Then, finally, Berenice sat down at a sidewalk café. And Stacey had the chutzpah to sit down at the next table.

The waiter took Berenice's order, then Stacey's, who, needing a boost to her courage, decided on a beer despite it being early in the day. Stacey sat there, staring straight ahead behind her dark glasses, trying to work up her courage yet not even daring to glance over at Berenice.

She probably should have.

Berenice took her phone out of her purse and typed a message into it, hitting "send" with a little flourish. Immediately, Stacey's phone beeped in her handbag. Berenice frowned. Before Stacey could reach her phone, Berenice typed another message and hit send again. Again, Stacey's phone beeped, this time in her hand. Berenice looked directly at her now and started typing again.

Stacey was going to need to think fast. She couldn't confront Berenice now; she was flustered and had yet to down her liquid courage. She hadn't retroplanned for this!

She made a show of peering at her screen then exclaiming, "Kids! Can't leave them alone for a minute."

From the corner of her eye, Stacey saw Berenice looking at her. No, studying her. Stacey pretended to type something in her phone when, in fact, she switched her phone into airplane mode, seconds before Berenice hit send yet again.

At the same moment, the waiter brought their orders. As he leaned over to place Berenice's cup on the table, someone walked into the café behind him and jostled him ever so slightly, ruining the perfect equilibrium of the *garçon*'s tray. The tall glass with Stacey's beer slid, slowly at first then gaining speed, tipping the tray and spilling onto the table and into Berenice's purse. Fifty centiliters was a lot of beer, especially when it was inside a Chanel handbag. Stacey was surprised to note that Chanel bags, with their superior craftsmanship, were watertight. Instead of seeping out through the fabric and the seams, the half-liter of beer stayed inside. Berenice started fishing out her belongings and the waiter ran to bring towels to mop up the mess.

Stacey took advantage of the ensuing chaos to leave the café terrace discreetly, realizing she couldn't confront Berenice now. The image of the beer sliding off the tray came to mind again. She had watched it like a car crash, in slow motion, knowing what was going to happen, not able to intervene. Stacey laughed to herself. Who was she kidding? She wouldn't have intervened, even if she could.

15

Rehaul

ON THE WAY HOME, Stacey replayed the scene in her head, again and again, torn between disap-pointment that she hadn't confronted Berenice and hilarity that Berenice got hers all the same. She had spent the morning studying Berenice at close quarters and saw that Berenice was more *coquette* and took better care of her appearance than Stacey did. She had to admit, she had gotten a bit lazy, a bit complacent.

What was it her friend Patricia had said? Some new

clothes, a make-over, a new hairstyle. She had to admit she could do with a rehaul.

When she got off the freeway, instead of turning right to go home, Stacey suddenly turned left to go to the nearest shopping mall. Once inside, she realized it had been a long time since she had been there. A lot of the stores were new; the décor had changed. *When did this happen?* she thought. She headed to her favorite store, something for women her age or maybe a little older, only to discover it no longer existed. In its place was a trendy boutique catering to a clientele both younger and more stylish than she. Although she had to admit she liked that dress in the window. The belt on the other mannequin was nice, too. But she couldn't go into that boutique. It wasn't for her.

The French have a great expression, *prendre son courage à deux mains*, which means literally "take your courage with your two hands." Or, as Nike said, "Just do it." Stacey hesitated, admiring the store window, reluctant to enter, then took the plunge. She quickly crossed the short distance between her and the inside of the store and felt the same shock as diving into a cold swimming pool on a hot summer day. Go fast or you never will.

She found herself nose to nose with Corinne, according to her name tag, a young shop girl, not much older than her daughter. The girl looked about as surprised as Stacey felt, then recovered and asked in a professional tone, "May I help you?"

"Yes, I'd like to update my clothes. It's been some time since I've gone shopping," Stacey replied. The girl nodded, knowingly. Clearly she had been thinking something along those lines, although possibly a bit more insulting if she was anything like Laura. Stacey continued, "I like the dress you have in the window. I think it would suit my figure...." Her voice trailed off. She felt so unsure.

The shop girl studied her from head to toe, then gave a nod of approval. "You're in good shape for someone your age. You'll look good in that dress. Come over here to the dressing room and I'll get the dress for you. What size?"

Stacey followed her to the fitting rooms, happy to let this girl take charge. She tried on the dress, first in the size she had asked for and then the smaller size that the girl had "taken the liberty" of bringing. It fit like a glove. She came out of the dressing room, modeling for the shop girl, studying herself from all angles, happy and surprised with the result.

"You don't think it's too young?" she asked. "I don't want to look like I'm trying to be a teenager again. Or like mutton dressed as lamb."

The girl looked puzzled. The English expression clearly didn't translate well, so Stacey explained that it referred to ladies who could not admit they are getting older and so dress in clothes that are far too young for them, the result being sad more than anything else.

The girl laughed and shook her head no. "You look hot. I wish my mom looked like you." The girl blushed, realizing what she had just said, then added "Do you just want the dress? Or can I bring you some other ideas?"

"That would be good," Stacey replied, still admiring herself in the dress, flattered and touched by the salesgirl's words.

For the next hour, Corinne, brought her various clothes, having her try on the "big pieces" then mixing and matching skirts, blouses, sweaters, leather pants (Leather pants! She could hardly believe it). Accessorizing. The two chatted and giggled like old friends, as Stacey decided to take three full outfits plus an extra blouse, which Corinne assured her would "work well" with her jeans.

As Stacey was paying, the young woman looked at her shyly then said, "Would you mind if I made another suggestion?"

"Corinne, I've had so much fun with you, you can tell me anything you want."

"I think you should change your hair." Seeing approval on Stacey's face, she continued, "I bet a few highlights would make all the difference. My friend Annie does a really good job with color. Do you want me to call her?" Stacey nodded yes.

Corinne whipped out her mobile phone, punched a number, said a few things to Annie presumably, turned back to Stacey, "Do you have time right now?" Again, Stacey nodded yes. Like the swimming pool, dive in before she chickened out. Corinne talked a bit more, hung up, and then went to find the other shop girl. "Can I take a break now?"

Stacey picked up her packages while Corinne clocked out, then the two walked through the mall, over to Annie at the hair stylists salon. Along the way, Corinne pointed out various shoes and jewelry that would go well with the items Stacey had just purchased. When they entered the salon, another young woman ran to greet them, shaking Stacey's hand and kissing Corinne on both cheeks. The girls settled Stacey into a chair, put the protection sheet on her, and started discussing Stacey's hair in an animated and technical manner, making her realize that here, too, times had changed. After a heated debate, the two girls came to an agreement and proposed their idea to Stacey: blond and chestnut highlights to brighten and soften her color, a cut slightly shorter and slightly more layered but above all much more modern than her current cut plus a re-structuring of her eyebrows and make-up in a brighter palette.

"You can do all that here?"

"No," Corinne answered, "but our friend Françoise works at Sephora. When you finish here, I'll come back and take you to Françoise."

"That's very sweet of you, but why are you doing all this for me?"

Corinne and Annie looked at each other, then Corinne replied "All day long, we see women like you, like our mothers, who could look really good if only they tried. We have all kinds of ideas for them, for better clothes and better hair. You're the first one who actually listened."

Stacey was surprised. She had done nothing unusual; she had simply paid attention, something these girls were clearly craving. In the pay attention/*faire attention* debate, this proved the theory that there is, indeed, a return on investment.

Stacey took Corinne's hand and gave it a squeeze before Annie shooed her away, saying "Come back at 3:00. And prepare to be dazzled."

16

Other men

AS STACEY PREPARED to walk from the shopping mall to the parking lot, she stopped short at the doors. Her hands were so full of shopping bags—she hadn't bought this much in years—that she couldn't push the door open. She started shifting bags from here to there, trying to free up a hand, when a masculine voice said "Here, let me get that for you."

She felt the person brush past her, through the door. She looked up from her purchases to see a man, tall, dark, about her age, holding the door for her. And ogling. As he held the door, he was looking her up and down.

Stacey blushed. *Must be Corinne and the girls' handiwork*, she thought. She passed through the door, murmuring her thanks.

"My pleasure," he replied with a smile.

Stacey put her purchases in the trunk, got in the car and decided to swing by the supermarket to pick up something easy for dinner. A rotisserie chicken, sauté some tomatoes and onions before adding to frozen green beans transforming them into *haricots verts à la grecque,* pre-washed green salad (how lazy was that?). She was in the wine section, debating between a classic white or a light red, when a deep voice interrupted her. "I see you've got the same dilemma I do," he said.

She looked up to see the man who went with the voice. Ten years younger than Stacey, blond, seriously built, with rugged good looks, as they say in the romance novels. She must have looked surprised, because he hurried to add, "Do I choose a white, which is the usual choice for poultry? Or do I go with a red, since I'm cooking the chicken in a spicy sauce?"

This seemed like a typical pick-up line but what the hell. He was cute; her husband was cheating.

"Spicy. Do you meant hot? Like chilis? Or full of

spice, like cumin or turmeric?"

"I do like things hot," he answered, winking at her.

Antonio—she quickly learned he was named after his mother's Italian grandfather—was planning to make *poulet basquaise*, a recipe Stacey knew well. Pieces of chicken are simmered in a sauce of tomatoes, green and red peppers and onion that are sliced into long thing slivers and pre-cooked in olive oil before adding the chicken and tomato. The peppers end up meltingly soft yet added texture to the dish because of their rope-like size.

The spice to which Antonio referred was from the garlic, of course, and also the *piment d'espelette*, a small red chili pepper native to the Basque Region, the area which was partially in France, partially in Spain, reaching from the Atlantic Coast into the mountainous Pyrenées. Years ago, Stacey and Jean had spent a vacation in Biarritz, the most famous of the cities in the *Pays Basque*.

Antonio broke into her reminiscences by saying that he loved to cook, to try new recipes, but was never completely sure of the wine choices and had yet to find good advice.

"People," he said, looking straight into her eyes, "can be so conventional."

Inwardly, Stacey screamed to herself, like a teenager at a Justin Bieber concert, loving the innuendo and the attention.

"A dish with such a depth of flavor deserves something full-bodied." There! She gave him her own innuendo. "You could go with a Saint Emilion." She carefully studied the bottles lined up on the shelves, all the while feeling Antonio studying her. "Ah,..." Stacey reached out and picked up a bottle, an Irouleguy Rouge, produced in the Basque Region, a less obvious choice but very, very good.

She handed him the bottle, returning his deep gaze, feeling a flutter, a thrill, a hint of something that just might... Someone else came into the wine aisle, the moment was lost, and Stacey headed to the check-out counter, leaving a missed opportunity? -- or a lovely flirt? --behind her. She had forgotten how good it felt, these little attentions from unknown men.

As she left the supermarket, the muzak played "It's Raining Men." *Exactly*, she thought.

17

Amélie and Laura

I T DIDN'T HAPPEN too often, but every now and then Stacey took a break from life. The beer in Berenice's handbag, Stacey's new clothes, the man flirting in the supermarket. It had been a good day and she was going to continue to enjoy it.

She brought her cosmopolitan and book to the living room sofa and settled in, feet up on the coffee table, drink on the end table. She opened the novel to where she had left off, took a sip of the cosmo, and started reading. She loved to read. She remembered her amazement in college when she learned that the faculty would actually give her a diploma for doing what she loved most, and so chose English as her major. Some weeks she had been "required" to read as many as three novels. The other students complained; she couldn't believe her good luck. Decades later, she was still reading, although the pace had slowed, especially since the kids were born and Jean did less and less to help at home. Even so, she averaged three novels a month, sometimes more.

Her favorite genre, although it wasn't officially a genre, was what she called "a book within a book," although a "story within a story" was probably more accurate since her first experience was with *Midsummer Night's Dream* and the bumbling craftsmen who put on a play for the king and queen.

The novel she was currently enjoying was entitled *The Reader of the 6:27*, the story of a young man who worked in a factory pulping books, who actually ran the huge machine which shredded ton after ton of books. He was required to crawl inside the machine every day for maintenance and took advantage of this time to steal the individual pages he found stuck there, pages which he read aloud every morning on the 6:27 train on his way to work. One day he found a memory stick in the train. When he opened it up, he discovered 72 word documents, the musings of a Madame Pipi, the cleaning lady in a public toilet somewhere, which read as a novel. Little by little, the man fell in love with the author of the vignettes. The novel, the one Stacey was reading, not the novel within, alternated the young man's story with Madame Pipi's writings. Rather, *Mademoiselle* Pipi's writings, for Stacey learned that she was 28 and single.

Stacey arrived at a passage in which Mademoiselle Pipi described, in great detail, one of her clients, if you can use that term for someone who dirtied the stall without even once leaving her a tip. "The fat man from 10 am," as she named him, never said hello or acknowledged her existence in any way. Every day, he came into the restroom at 10 sharp, to stall number 8. If it wasn't free, he would wait until it was, even if all the other stalls were available. Stacey took a sip of her cosmo and laughed to herself. She knew people like that.

Once ensconced in stall 8, the fat man would do what he'd come there for, use a huge amount of toilet paper, at least half a roll, then leave the premises—unflushed. With no tip in Mademoiselle Pipi's little tip jar.

Every day, Mademoiselle Pipi was obliged to go into stall 8, flush the toilet, scrub it, and replace the roll of TP, all for no money whatsoever. It made her furious, so furious in fact that she wanted revenge. One day, at 9:45, she replaced the toilet paper with an empty roll, taping just enough TP to peek through the bottom of the dispenser to make it appear that all was well. Her friend whom she included in the plot stayed in stall 8 until the fat man appeared, always punctual, at 10 am. The friend left the stall, the fat man rushed in and the remaining description made Stacey laugh until she had to put down the novel and dry her eyes. She just couldn't shake the image of the fat man seated on the throne, pants down at his ankles, pulling on the TP, discovering his dilemma and not daring to call out for help. As she savored the image, the fat man's face morphed into Jean's; the public restroom stall into the "little corner" in Christophe's apartment. She laughed even harder.

Just then, the front door opened and Laura walked in, her eyes darting from her mother laughing alone to the book splayed face down on the sofa and the empty cocktail glass on the end table. "Hey Mom, you OK?"

"A-OK," answered Stacey. She had had such a good laugh, she wanted more. "You want to watch a movie?"

"Now? You usually make me do my homework first," answered Laura, not sure what to make of this.

"Homework, schmomework," laughed Stacey, albeit a little drunkenly. She wasn't used to drinking in the afternoon; it definitely put a rosy edge on things. "You choose the movie, I'll make the popcorn," she said and hurried into the kitchen. She put the bag of popcorn into the microwave and, as she waited for the popping to finish, noticed all the fixings for the cosmopolitan still on the counter, a sort of invitation.

By the time Laura came in to show her the DVD she had chosen, Stacey had mixed another cocktail and was pouring a pink liquid from the shaker into two cocktail glasses. Two! She handed the one that was only half full to Laura, took the other glass in one hand, the popcorn bowl in the other, and headed to the living room, leaving the dirty dishes in the sink, the vodka, Cointreau and cranberry juice bottles and lime remains strewn over the countertop, something she usually found unacceptable.

"You don't want to straighten up first?" Laura asked, following her mother.

"Not really. Do you?"

"Yeah, right," Laura laughed.

"What movie did you choose, dear?" Stacey inquired.

"*Amélie*," answered Laura.

"Good choice," Stacey answered.

"You're not going to make us watch something else?"

Usually, there were interminable discussions over what movie to watch, Stacey always preferring something artsy or, worse, foreign, in its native language with subtitles. Laura usually countered with "Who wants to *read* a movie?" The conversation then escalated to argument, hurt feelings and banging doors.

"No, you made a good choice," Stacey answered, raising her glass in a mock toast.

As the movie progressed, the mother and daughter sitting side by side, companionably sharing the popcorn and laughing at the dysfunctional wait staff in the restaurant where Amélie works or the running joke about her father's garden gnome traveling the world, Stacey wondered how long it had been since she had so completely enjoyed just being with her daughter. Adolescence was hard on mothers.

When they got to the scene where Amélie decided to take revenge on the grocer, Stacey was suddenly jolted alert.

On her way down the apartment building's stairs, Amélie discovered the grocer's keys in his front door. She took them, meaning to return them to him as she passed by his shop. When she arrived at the store, however, the grocer was making jokes to his customers at the expense of his shop boy, a young man who was handicapped both physically and mentally. Amélie was angered by his cruelty and decided to get revenge. She made copies of the keys and put the original back in the front door. *Ni vu, ni connu.*

Not seen, not known. Later, she entered the grocer's apartment with her set of keys, looked around, and went from room to room, moving things here and there.

Cut to a close-up of Amélie, the film suddenly in black and white, Amélie dressed all in black, black gloves, black mask covering most of her face, a black Spanish gaucho hat on her head. One arm was raised behind her to counterbalance the sword in her other hand and, swish, swish, swish, she marked the Z for Zorro on the grocer's door. Zorro, upholder of the law, protector of the innocent, righter of wrongs.

Stacey put the movie on pause, rummaged through her purse for her phone, and started typing furiously: make copy of keys, alarm clock, whiskey...

"Geez, Mom," Laura complained. "Can we just watch the movie?"

Stacey punched the remote and the movie started up again. Several scenes later Stacey and Laura saw the results of Amélie's mischief. Stacey continued to take notes on her phone.

Laura took the remote control and hit pause. "Do you have to do that now?" she asked. "It's really rude."

"Like when you text at the dinner table?" Stacey answered, mid-stroke.

Laura said nothing, unpausing the movie and staring

straight ahead at the screen.

Although Stacey and Laura laughed together at the grocer getting his just deserts, and sighed together when Amelie found true love, the easy camaraderie they had been feeling with one another was gone.

18

Bachelor pad sabotage

THE NEXT DAY felt like a hangover, and not just because she had had too many cosmos the day before.

Despite her success sabotaging lunch at La Trattoria or the cancellation email from the spa at *Perros-Guerrec*, Stacey kept thinking about the text, "We'll stop by Christophe's afterward." She kept hearing the words in her head and, with each repetition, grew angrier and angrier. Christophe had never liked her. He had never accepted their marriage, let alone supported it. She wasn't at all surprised that he let Jean use his apartment to do his dirty deeds. And Jean. What a cheapskate! He didn't even spring for a nice hotel and room service. She tried to do the dishes to distract herself but instead kept thinking how Christophe's apartment was *their* special place. She could see Jean bringing his favorite whiskey or, maybe, a bottle of champagne for them to share. Berenice would bring flowers or a scented candle to leave her mark. With each of their meetings, they would bring and leave a little something until the apartment reflected them more than Christophe and become a place they shared.

Stacey came back to herself, realizing she had been scrubbing the same plate for the last ten minutes. She put it back in the soapy dishwater then rinsed and dried her hands.

Just like *Amélie*, the first step was to find the key and make a copy. Easy peasy, for Christophe had left them a key in case anything needed tending while he was away. It should be hanging on the key rack in the entryway. Yes, there it was. Evidently Jean was putting it back in between his trysts. She pocketed the key, got her handbag and went to the mall to get a copy made and to pick up a few items to help her imitate *Amélie le justicier*.

Since Jean had left the key, that meant he wasn't planning on going there today, so it would be a good time to do her dastardly deeds. She drove the 15 km to Paris, to the rue de Bourgogne where Christophe's apartment was. 15 km sounds far, farther than the actual 9.3 miles to the neighborhood ensconced between the Invalides where Napoleon was buried, the Musée Rodin and, toward the Seine, the Assemblée Nationale, the French equivalent of Capitol Hill. If she continued to the Assemblée Nationale then followed the Seine east for a few blocks, she would reach the Musée d'Orsay, famous for its collection of impressionist art.

It was a very desirable location. She had to admit—Christophe had made a wise investment when he bought here.

Stacey was lucky; she found a parking spot on the rue de Bourgogne itself, just a hundred meters down the street from the lovers' nest. She wouldn't have to carry her supplies far.

She had seldom gone to Christophe's apartment and had forgotten what a peaceful, masculine place it was. As she walked in the door, she noted the parquet floors, the Persian carpet in the living room, the leather sofa, the high-tech stereo. Very manly. Very nice.

Stacey crossed the room to the stereo, one of those with a slot to place your smart phone and play your library of songs over the high end speakers. Sabotage here was easy enough. She turned the volume dial all the way up. Since the markings on the stereo were black on black, she didn't think Jean would notice, not until he played the first song, that is. She moved to the cocktail cabinet, took out the bottle of whiskey, Jean's brand, so probably something he had brought. She took the salt and chopstick from her supply bag, carefully poured the salt into the whiskey, stirred with the chopstick, put the cap back on, still saw the grains of salt so shook the bottle, and peered into the amber liquid again. Satisfied, she put the bottle back in the cabinet and walked to the bathroom where she found the hot water heater and flipped the switch to off. She pocketed the toothpaste and replaced it with a tube of diaper cream, carefully positioning the label downward against the shelf. Straight from *Amélie*. From the bathroom, to the toilet. Borrowing this time from Mademoiselle Pipi, she unrolled the entire roll, leaving just two of the perforated sheets before replacing the roll in its dispenser, giving the illusion that all was well. She found the extra rolls and plopped them into her supply bag.

She moved on to the bedroom, the true "scene of the crime" in her mind. Again, she paused as she admired the room. Christophe really did have good taste, despite aiding and abetting an adulterer. The tall windows gave good natural light. With the hardwood floors, the king size bed, the walls and bedspread in beiges and browns with just a hint of color in the pillows, she wondered how a room could feel so good and yet be used to hurt her so much. Stacey tried to shake off this sentimentality.

Don't think, do, she scolded herself.

She got down on all fours and looked under the bed. Quite a few dust bunnies, which meant that the cleaning lady, if there was one, didn't go there too often. This fit Stacey's plans exactly. She took two bunches of bananas from her bag of tricks and placed them under the bed, pushing them to the middle with her foot. On the internet, she had read that rotting bananas attract massive numbers of fruit flies. A cloud of fruit fries was sure to kill the mood!

In case it didn't, or in case the internet was wrong, she went to mood-killer-number-two. She took a black lace thong—not hers!—from her supply bag along with a tube of hair gel. She rinsed the thong in water in the bathroom, spread hair gel over the crotch of it, rinsed her hands and, carrying it with the chopstick, brought it back to the bedroom.

She folded down the duvet (*quelle snobberie!*) and sheet, positioned the slimy underwear in the middle, two thirds of the way down, then carefully folded the covers back in place, arranging them exactly as she had found them.

Turning to leave the room, she saw a clock radio on the night table and thought again of *Amélie*. She sat down on the bed to study the clock radio, then pushed "time set" and the "+" button. Suddenly, it was one and a half hours later. Would this prank work like in the movie? Would they think they were late and hurry off?

Next, the kitchen. Opening the fridge, she saw three bottles of champagne were chilling. Good champagne, too. Stacey took them out, set them on the floor next to a bunch of liter-sized Perrier bottles and put three of the water bottles in the fridge, in their place. When you're expecting romantic champagne, a Perrier toast would be disappointing, one more piece of sand jamming the gears of their tryst.

Last, but not least, she took a mouse trap out of her supply bag along with the stink bomb bag which she had carefully protected in a little box. She chuckled to herself. All that web research to create this little gem. Stacey attached the bag to the mouse trap, just as she had seen in the YouTube video, set the mouse trap then carefully placed the mouse trap in the bottom of the garbage can, under a paper towel.

Blasting music. Salted whiskey. No more toilet paper. Fruit flies under the bed. Someone else's dirty panties in the bed. No cold champagne. No hot water. Time flying, or at least appearing to. A stink bomb the lovers would set off themselves. Amélie would be proud.

19

Go big

LIKE ALL JUNKIES, her high, that sweet, sweet note of revenge mingled with victory and self-satisfaction for her cleverness, was quickly followed by a crash which left her down, morose, dissatisfied without knowing why, possibly because she didn't really know why she was doing all this in the first place.

The more she did, the more the cycle sped up, so much so that she hardly even waited for results before jumping back in again.

She had stopped cleaning the house. She barely made meals anymore. All her energy went into stalking Berenice and concocting little revenge ploys, yet she always felt distracted, brooding, something nagging at her but she couldn't quite put her finger on it.

There's one way to solve that, Stacey thought. She had to go big. She had to something so horrible it would break them up for good.

A man's Achilles' heel is actually about 36 inches higher. Insult his virility and you've insulted him. Irreparably.

She grabbed her handbag which she had left in the kitchen and noticed last night's dishes and this morning's coffee cups piled in the sink. Heading to the door, she saw Jean's sweater strewn on the sofa, and the DVDs someone had taken out and left on the coffee table. She was in a hurry and would do take care of all that later, she thought, although, given the layer of dust on the living room furniture, this must not be the first time she vowed to take care of it later.

Right now, she had a mission. She locked the door and headed to the train station.

Her friend Isabelle had talked about a sex shop near Montparnasse that was "really nice, not sleazy at all." Hard to imagine a sex shop which wasn't sleazy but she'd just have to trust Isabelle on this one. She'd buy some Viagra—or whatever OTC equivalent the store had—and leave it in the lovers' nest with a little note, "Jean, let's spice things up a little." Or—oh my God! What if she also bought a dildo then an ambiguous note which made him feel he wasn't satisfying Berenice. She chuckled to herself, then checked herself. She didn't want to act like a crazy woman in her own neighborhood. She was still smiling to herself, though, as she boarded the train and found a seat. Paris bound.

Along the way, the train came to a halt at one of the stations. There was a demolition site next to the train station, the old-fashioned kind with a giant crane and wrecking ball. In the few minutes it took for the passengers to board, she saw the crane turn, swing the wrecking ball back then forward again, crashing into the side of the building, splintering the side wall, people's ruined lives, crashing to the ground.

The back wall was plumb against the next building. On it, she could see the outline of the different floors, the different rooms on each level, one here with wallpaper with an old-fashioned flower motif. Chrysanthemums? Maybe. There, a subdued stripe on a beige background. It was strangely reminiscent of those photos of Hiroshima, after the nuclear bomb, where human forms left charred silhouettes on the buildings left intact by the blast.

It was oddly disturbing.

The train started up again, arriving at her favorite part of the trip, wiping away the melancholy left by the demolition site. Now, for a few precious minutes, there were no buildings nor trees, and from the vantage point of the train tracks, you could see La Défense, Montmartre, the new Vuitton Museum, Montparnasse and the Eiffel Tower, a panorama of Paris with the *Dame de Fer* smack dab in the middle. She had seen this view a hundred times and was always stunned by the beauty.

Then, the train passed into a tunnel and the magic was gone.

A change in trains at La Défense, a few minutes on the metro, she arrived at the Montparnasse station, and headed to the rue d'Odessa.

A few streets down, in the middle of the block, was the store. Discreet, it was not. A big fuchsia sign over glass doors, mannequins to the left and right of the door modeling lingerie, more or less exotic, more or less fabric. To the left of that, a big glass window showing off a display of creams, sprays, games and contraptions. Yes, 'contraption' was probably the right word to describe the immense variety of gadgets, some of which she wasn't sure what part of the anatomy was targeted.

She looked past the window display into the store, aisle after aisle of merchandise organized into departments much like a supermarket. The bright lighting was reminiscent of a supermarket as well. Isabelle was right. It wasn't sleazy; it was functional, which was perhaps even more disconcerting.

She stood in front of the store trying to get her nerve up to go inside. And couldn't. She just couldn't. There was something upsetting about the normality of this shop. Maybe she would have preferred something more secretive, a little more sordid. A blacked out front window, dim lighting, plain packages without the graphic descriptions of how you will drive your lady crazy tonight.

The fact of the matter was this whole revenge thing wasn't working. She schemed, she executed her plans, had some fun wreaking a little havoc, and then they made up again. She was no good at this. She had bought a secret phone. She had become a stalker, for God's sake, and still things were fine between Jean and Berenice. They were more resilient than she had thought. Maybe if she were meaner. Maybe if ... no. That was not who she was.

There, on the sidewalk in front of the lurid shop window, Stacey realized that she wasn't mean enough to do the really horrible things it would take to be effective. She wouldn't—couldn't – shame them publicly with billboards,

Facebook or whatever, and as a result her silly little mischief would never be anything more than mosquitos, annoyances the illicit couple could easily swat away.

What was it Jean had said on the phone to Berenice that night? That Stacey was good with the house and kids, but not capable of more. Maybe he was right after all.

She felt as if the other people walking down the street were judging her, snickering at this middle-aged housewife paralyzed by the lure/repulsion of this temple of sex, or maybe they could see her for the loser she was, unable to do anything definitive to defend her family. She turned back toward the metro, dejected.

She was incapable of going big so she would just go home.

Part II

"L'avenir d'un enfant est l'œuvre de sa mère."
- Napoléon Bonaparte

A child's future is
his mother's handicraft.

1

The intervention

DEPRESSED. DEJECTED. Stacey arrived home feeling she had hit rock bottom. She opened the front door only to find Laura and David sitting together at the kitchen table, each fiddling with the mug of tea in front of them, looking worried. They looked like an old married couple, worried about their daughter who missed her curfew and so must be turning bad.

David took charge. "Mom," he said, "can you sit down for a few minutes? We want to talk with you." He gestured to the chair between them, looking solemn.

"Of course dear," she replied, sitting.

"We're worried about you," he continued.

"Worried? Why?"

He gestured to the sink filled with dirty dishes, the bread and jam left on the countertop where someone had served himself for breakfast and never put it away. She saw where this was going.

Oh my God, she thought. *An intervention!* After all she had been through that day and her kids staged an intervention? Despite her hurt, she suppressed a laugh. David's solemnity was laughable, but she didn't want him to have hurt feelings too.

"You're worried about *me* because *you* don't clean up after yourselves?" Her voice came out sharper than she had expected, catching all three of them by surprise. He looked away.

Laura came to his rescue.

"You've made a fair point. We really should help out more. Both of us. But we're still worried about you. The house is all messy. You've stopped cooking. We find you on the computer at all hours. You leave early. You come home late. You even went out on a school night."

Ah, the opera, Stacey thought.

"You've changed your clothes and your hair ...." She

paused for a moment. "OK, I have to admit, I like your new clothes, and your hair and make-up are cool. But, still, it's not like you. It's like you don't care about anything anymore." Laura's voice trailed off before she blurted out. "Are you having an affair?"

The children's faces, because they really did look like small children at that moment, looked so fearful and so vulnerable, so very different from the blasé teenagers who irritated her daily. She laughed out loud.

"No!" she cried. The irony! She spent her time tracking down and torturing her husband's hussy and the kids accused *her* of having an affair. She laughed again. "Of course not!"

The kids looked relieved by her frank reaction, then Laura began again. "So what's going on? Why all the changes?"

What could she tell them? That their father was having an affair and she had become obsessed with getting revenge? That revenge, like crack, was an addiction which could take over your life? That she wasn't even good at it. That she was a loser. That ... no, none of that would do. They were still her children and she must protect them.

She took a deep breath.

"You know, you two are growing up. You're no longer babies. You don't need me taking care of you all the time.

You've both been telling me this for a long time, not just since I've been ... preoccupied," she paused, looking at both kids who nodded in agreement. "I can admit that, in the past, I've been too present. I heard your complaints and have tried to step back, to give you more space to live your lives, to stop being so involved. Maybe I haven't known how to let go gracefully."

David cut her off. "So you decided not to be involved at all?" He looked hurt.

Stacey took another deep breath.

"I've been pursuing some of my own interests, which I haven't done in a long time. Laura has her music friends. David, you've got your computer stuff. It's normal that I have something, too." Here, too, she needed to proceed carefully, not wanting to specify that her new hobbies were harassment and revenge. "Maybe I've gone overboard, gone too far the other way." David looked relieved. Laura nodded in agreement. "Maybe, too, I need your help now. What if you guys helped more around the house, so I could have time to do my own thing and give you more space?"

The kids took the opening. Together, they discussed what they liked (home-cooked meals, feeling someone cared about them), what they didn't like (mess all over the house, Stacey giving them the third degree over every little thing), what Stacey liked (having real conversations with her family, having time for herself), what she didn't like (everyone expecting her to clean up after them). The kids offered suggestions on what they could all do differently, where they could compromise, where one of them would just have to "suck it up" as David said. They even suggested outings they would like to do together, all three of them.

Stacey was thrilled. She made more tea for the three of them and brought out a box from the *Maison du Chocolat* from her secret stash to fuel more discussion, which morphed into each kid talking about what was going on in school just now, and their dreams for the future. Stacey was flabbergasted. The kids still needed her, but differently from before. They wanted to share their ideas with her just as much as she wanted them to, and in the space of a few minutes they had created a roadmap for building a better relationship.

2

Planning for the weekend

FRIDAY CAME, the day Jean was to leave for his weekend away. Stacey watched as he packed a small suitcase, asking him questions about the company team-building exercises, listening to his answers, all lies, which came with such ease. She felt like a cat playing with a mouse; she knew he planned to spend the weekend with Berenice and not with his colleagues. She also knew that he didn't know—didn't even suspect—that she had cancelled his reservations.

Jean gave her a kiss, a surprisingly romantic one given

the circumstances, and said he would be back Sunday evening.

Sunday evening? Stacey asked herself. If her plan worked, he would be home by Saturday morning. *How would he explain that?* she wondered.

If it worked, they'd turn around and drive back to Paris during the night. If it didn't work, if the hotel still had the room available, they'd be set for the weekend. In any case, nothing would happen until midnight, when the illicit couple arrived at the hotel. Stacey could wait at home—but she knew she would spend her time watching the clock. Brooding.

The French had a great expression: *tromper l'ennui.* *Tromper* meant to make a mistake or to deceive. Ironically, it was often used for someone in exactly the same situation as Stacey, *la femme trompée.* *L'ennui* means boredom, so together the phrase meant to conquer one's boredom.

That was what she would do.

Stacey called out to her kids. "David, Laura. Could you come here for a few minutes?" What if she started applying some of the things they had discussed in her "intervention"?

The kids grumbled, as teenagers do, but came to the kitchen anyway, ready for school. "I can't be late, Mom," said Laura. "Math quiz."

"Yeah, she's got a rendezvous with destiny," snickered David, alluding to Laura's poor math skills.

Before Laura could complain about his snide remark, Stacey replied, "I saw how hard you studied. I know you'll do well." She gave Laura a little hug. "That's not what I wanted to talk about. Since Dad's away for the weekend, what about doing some of those outings we talked about? We've got tonight, Saturday and Sunday until dinnertime. Three days. Three of us. How about each of us chooses one thing to do? You should still have enough time to do your homework and see your friends."

Immediately the kids started giving suggestions then discussing the merits of the different ideas. As the level of excitement grew, Stacey broke in. "We don't have to decide now. And Laura's got that quiz. Why don't we meet up here after school and finalize our plans then?" The kids nodded. "Besides, that'll give us all time to think about what we want to do most."

On that note the kids left. Clearly, they were going to talk about weekend options all the way to school. *A good way to trick Laura's math anxiety*, thought Stacey.

As the door closed behind them, Stacey started straightening the living room, picking up a discarded candy wrapper, fluffing a pillow, running the dust rag over the flat surfaces. She caught herself humming a happy tune and realized that right then, right in that moment, she was happy. She was making the home cozy and welcoming for her family. She was going to share some fun with her kids, experiences she hoped would allow her to know them better as young adults. She wasn't thinking about Jean nor his slut. She was too busy deciding what outing *she* wanted to do with the kids.

When the kids came home, they were met with the smell of fresh-baked cookies.

"Yum, my favorites," said David as he took a snickerdoodle off the plate.

"Wow!" said Laura, taking a cookie too. "It's been ages since you baked cookies. What a treat!"

"I decided to clean the house today," replied Stacey, serving herself as well, "but there wasn't a whole lot to do. Hardly anything to pick up. And your bathroom was already clean." Laura looked proud. Her mom had noticed. "With all that extra time, I felt like making cookies."

It was a salesman's old trick, salesman, teacher, B.F. Skinner's when working with his pigeons: reward good behavior with a treat in order to reinforce that behavior and have more of it in the future. That wasn't why Stacey had baked the cookies, however. She was honestly happy that the kids had taken their discussion seriously and were doing their share, so she wanted to do her part, too.

"Have you thought about what you want to do?" Stacey handed the plate around. Once the kids had taken some cookies and given her the plate back, Laura began.

"I want to go to the *Centre Pompidou*."

"A museum?" retorted David. "Bo-ring! No way I'm gonna go."

Before Laura could come back with an insult and the whole thing escalated, Stacey jumped in. "You know, David," she paused to dip her cookie into her tea, letting it soak up some of the liquid, adding to the deliciousness. She did this slowly, purposefully, to show she was thinking through what she would say next. "You know, you might want to wait before refusing, because if you refuse Laura's outing, she might just refuse yours—and then where will we be?"

Given the look on his face, David clearly hadn't thought that far ahead. In a mimic of his mother, he dunked a cookie into his cup of tea and said, "Ok, I'll wait. Tell us more, Laura."

And Laura did. She explained that the *Centre Pompidou* had an expo of the artist César. She described his work and said she had been interested by him for quite some time now.

Stacey was amazed. She hadn't known.

David just said "The giant metal thumb guy? OK. That could be cool. Museums are open during the day, right?"

Again, Stacey was amazed, but not for the same reason. "Yes, museums are generally open during the day. Why?"

"Because what I want to do is at night."

"What do you want to do?" asked Laura, a little worried.

Confidence reigns, thought Stacey.

"It's a movie," began David. "Some kids in my class were talking about it. It's supposed to be way cool..." He went to describe the movie, only he didn't know the name and all the popular kids seemed to have seen it. Stacey smiled to herself. Her techno-geek son secretly wanted to be one of the popular kids.

Evidently Laura was one of the "in group" because she said, "I heard of that. It's called *The Rocky Horror Picture Show*."

Stacey laughed out loud.

The kids turned and stared. "Have you heard of it, Mom?"

"Yes," she laughed. "I've heard of it." She thought of all those late-night sessions of the cult film in her youth.

"When is it playing?"

Laura was already on her phone, researching movie times and places. "It's on tonight. Paris 5th arrondissement. But it's kind of late. It won't start until 10 pm."

"That's perfect. We'll eat here, drive in to Paris and get there in time to get good seats. David's movie tonight, Laura's exhibition tomorrow. This is working out really well because what I wanted to do is on Sunday morning."

The happy look disappeared from Laura's face. David, crestfallen, whispered, "You're not going to make us go to church, are you?"

Again, Stacey laughed out loud. "Not church, silly. Brunch." Both kids let out a sigh of relief. "At the *Royal Monceau.*"

"No way!" exclaimed David.

"Oh my God!" Laura cried.

Stacey beamed. She had raised them well. Despite all the burgers and fries with their friends, these two were foodies at heart. They could appreciate the very best.

3

Rocky Horror

WHY DON'T WE prepare for the movie now, then you guys can get a start on your schoolwork before I make dinner?"

"What do you mean 'prepare for the movie'?" asked David. "Don't we just show up?"

"Trust me," Stacey smiled. Things had surely changed since her day but the basis still had to be there. She picked up three old newspapers she had left near the fireplace before heading toward the kitchen. "I'll toast the bread. David, do you still have your water pistols?" He looked puzzled but nodded yes. "Go get them. Three, if possible."

She turned to Laura. "You still smoking?" Laura opened her mouth as if to deny, but Stacey cut her off. "You use matches or lighters?"

"Lighter," Laura gasped.

"Excellent."

The kids exchanged looks. That was the last reaction they were expecting.

Stacey continued, "Go get three of them, if you have 'em."

She went to the kitchen and started toasting slices of white bread (*nasty stuff*, she thought), as the kids went to collect their assigned items and put them in Stacey's tote along with the newspapers and, little by little, the toast.

"David, be sure to fill the water guns. Laura—would you mind putting a handful of rice in a ziplock bag?"

"Do we need to cook it first?" asked Laura, starting to reach for a saucepan.

"No, sweetie. That would be weird."

The kids again exchanged looks, silently agreeing that this, already, was weird. Stacey looked through the contents of her tote bag as she deposited the last slice of toast. "Looks like we're good to go. Should we eat a little early, say 7:30?"

The kids agreed and she shooed them off to their

homework, calling out the old French adage, *Ce qui est fait, n'est plus à faire.* What is already done no longer needs to be done. A mere statement of the obvious while the American equivalent took a higher moral ground: Don't put off until tomorrow what you should do today.

In any case, it was the first time in years that neither kid argued over whether they really needed to do homework on a Friday afternoon. A few hours later, no one argued, either, over who would do the dishes after dinner. Everyone helped; while Stacey hand-washed the baking dish and the frying pan, David loaded the dishwasher and Laura wiped the table. In a matter of minutes, they were free to leave for Paris.

They drove in, parked the car, and walked a short distance to find a long line of people already waiting in front of the movie theatre. Some of the people were in costume, to Stacey's delight; some were from David's class, to his embarrassment. The line started to move and they slowly inched their way to the box office where Stacey purchased three tickets.

"Rice is forbidden," the vendor said. "Too much mess to clean up."

Stacey took the baggie of rice from her tote and laid it on the counter. "Why did you tell me and not the people ahead of us?"

"They're virgins. They don't know anything," he winked at Stacey as he said to the kids, "I'm glad to see you're in good hands for your first time," then turned to serve the next person in line.

The kids looked horrified.

Stacey looked at their faces and laughed. "Calm down," she said. "It's just the movie's lingo. The first time you see *Rocky Horror*, they call you a virgin. Nothing more to it than that." The kids sighed from relief, reassured nothing weird was going to happen, and pleased that their mom clearly knew what she was doing.

They entered the theater. Stacey saw David looking at his classmates, almost longingly, so she proposed that he go sit with them. "It'll be more fun than sitting with your mom," she said.

"I don't know," David replied, carefully studying the group. "No backpacks. The girls only have small handbags. They didn't bring any of the stuff you did."

"Yeah," added Laura. "I bet they're virgins and don't know anything." Stacey smiled.

The trio sat down together and enjoyed the show where as much happened in the room as on the screen. Stacey had to admit that the new generation of performers was very good, despite English being a foreign language for them. As the scenes progressed, Stacey handed out the supplies so that the kids were prepared for the rain, the toast, the song, "There's a light."

David leaned over to her and whispered, "Is it all bad puns like this?"

As soon as the small church appeared on screen, Stacey felt Laura take her hand and pour in a small amount of rice. Stacey looked at her wonderingly.

"I had put some in my pocket," whispered Laura. "Just in case."

Stacey chuckled, turned to David on her other side and gave him a little rice, too. Breaking the rules with your children-- now there was a new experience!

4

Centre Pompidou

SATURDAY MORNING, Stacey got up long before the kids did but, since they had gotten home around one, she decided to let them sleep in. When they did emerge, each carried a text book, not wanting to lose valuable time before their next outing. Not nagging her children to do their homework—again, a new experience for Stacey. One she was enjoying.

At the end of the morning there was still no sign of Jean. Stacey did what she could to push him from her thoughts and was about to start making lunch, when Laura came into the kitchen. "How about some help?"

"You don't have to," replied Stacey. "You've been studying all morning. You deserve a break."

"Yeah, but I saw you doing the laundry. You deserve a break, too." Laura reached into a cupboard and took out a large bowl. "Should I make salad?" Stacey nodded. "Balsamic or red wine vinegar for the vinaigrette?"

Stacey was flabbergasted, so much so that all she could answer was, "Up to you. You're the chef."

As Laura made the vinaigrette then started chopping raw vegetables for her salad, Stacey put the green beans on to cook and started to pound the chicken breasts to flatten them before browning in melted butter in a skillet.

"*Poulet paillarde?*" asked Laura. Stacey nodded, pleased with her daughter's culinary knowledge. When the chicken and butter started releasing a flavorful aroma, David sailed into the kitchen.

"Should I set the table here or in the dining room?"

Re-flabbergasted.

Stacey had spent years battling, then giving up all hope, of ever getting David to help out. And here he was, voluntarily, before she could even ask. She was so glad that the kids had staged their intervention.

When lunch was over and the clean-up done, Stacey

suggested they drive in to Paris and have a coffee before the expo.

"You know, Mom," began Laura, "we really should take the train. The museum is close to the metro stop, and it's much better for the planet."

"And you won't have to pay for parking," David chimed in. "With the money you save, you can buy us a dessert to go with that coffee."

Stacey laughed. "It's a deal."

So they trained into the city, changed to the RER A at *La Défense*, then straight sailing to *Châtelet Les Halles* from where a short walk took them to the *Centre Pompidou*. As Stacey stood in line, the kids mugged it up in front of the giant bronze thumb in the square, taking photos of one another, then a selfie of the two of them and the thumbnail, then another one of Laura kissing the thumb as it loomed over her. Stacey discreetly filmed them with her camera, getting so wrapped up with their antics that she was cut in front of several times. Standing in line—yet another cultural difference between French and Americans.

As she neared the security check, Stacey called to the kids who came running, opening coats and handbags to show the guard they were weaponless. From there, they purchased tickets then rode the escalators inside the giant colored tubes on the side of the building, all the way to the top floor and the temporary exhibition.

"Shall we have coffee now?" asked Stacey.

"How 'bout we wait?" David answered. "I'm interested in seeing what else this guy has done."

Stacey didn't know what was a bigger surprise, David showing an interest in art or David supporting his sister's initiative. The biggest surprise of all, however, came a few minutes later when they started looking at the pieces and Laura started telling them about Cesar's life and career, the different phases of his work, the different influences. She was very knowledgeable. And passionate. She told it all in such a way that Stacey was caught up in the story and wanted to know what happened next. David, too, was spellbound. Stacey was—proud? Yes, she was proud of her daughter but that wasn't all. She was discovering a whole new side of Laura. Stacey sincerely liked this new person she was meeting.

The César exhibition was interesting. The César exhibition, as told by Laura, was extraordinary. They saw tiny, delicate statues made by soldering pieces of scrap iron together: a rooster, France's national symbol; a pigeon; then, they saw more monumental pieces: a bat with a six-foot wingspan; an ostrich taller than a grown man, wings outstretched, on roller skates. Laura pointed out the wrench on the left leg and the old car part on the right.

"An ostrich Robocop!" David exclaimed, before trying to capture both the bird and himself in a selfie.

From there, they moved on to the expansions, works made by combining different chemicals which, when reacting together, created a mousse which later solidified. The result were ooey-gooey pieces Stacey did not care for, but the kids did. Laura, usually an underperformer in math and science, spouted off phrases like "polyurethane" "exothermic reaction" and "industrial chemistry." David was nodding in understanding.

After the expansions, they saw the compressions. César had experimented with many different "media" as Laura called it. As far as Stacey could see, "media" meant garbage: wooden fruit and vegetable crates all squished together to make a *tableau*, the rounded backs of *bistrot* chairs schmushed into a statue. Again, César's works progressed in size until Stacey and her kids saw themselves in front of a car, squashed flat like a bug, hanging vertically on the wall, then a second one, this time painted fire engine red after being flattened. You could see the roof, slightly further from the wall than the trunk and hood, the tire wells making two graceful curves on each side of the chassis.

David handed his phone to his sister. "Do you think

you can get it all in?" he asked, as he posed next to the car.

After the photo, the trio walked into the next room, where six metal pillars stood in two rows, heavy, metallic, massive, contrasting with the light wood flooring and the transparency of the floor-to-ceiling windows overlooking Paris. People strolled around them, studying each piece from all four sides before moving on to the next one. As they got closer, Stacey realized that these, too, were compressed cars, probably several cars per piece judging by the variety of colors and finishes. The pieces (statues? columns?) were large, almost as tall as Stacey. They felt solid and oddly appealing. As Stacey and the kids walked around them, she had a sudden flash.

Jean's convertible.

It was his baby, a sporty two-seater. He had bought the car saying that it would be for the two of them, so they could get away *en amoureux*, even if just for the day. The two of them, together, the top down, the wind in their hair, the sun on their faces, stopping for a romantic picnic on the beach, then a *sieste coquine,* a naughty nap, in the dunes. He had painted a tempting picture, they had bought the car, he complained that the fabric top was cold in winter, and they had never used it to get away together. Not even for a day. There was always a reason: the kids, a sick relative, a repairman coming to the house, Jean having too much work. She thought about that with sadness and regret. And realization. If Jean had so much work to catch up on during the weekend, it was because he did something else during the week.

In a flash, Stacey saw Jean's beloved convertible there, in that room with them, compressed into an *oeuvre d'art* that the Parisian intelligentsia was admiring. Jean, standing beside it, was torn between bereavement for his dear, dear car and pride from the snobs' admiration.

Lost in this image, Stacey came to a start when Laura gently touched her elbow. "Mom, are you OK? Since we've seen everything, David was suggesting we get coffee and dessert now. Can we? The café's that way."

"Of course, dear," Stacey answered, then followed her kids out, scolding herself silently. She had been having a lovely time with her kids, really lovely, and now she went and got lost in negative thoughts like that. Polluting her afternoon!

She sat down with the kids, ordered a tea and enjoyed listening to the two of them talk about the exhibition.

"I mean," said David, "can you really call it art when you're just using the car crusher in the junkyard?" Laura replied, the debate raged while Stacey marveled at her two teenagers discussing art in a Parisian café. In the back of her mind, though, was that vision of Jean's car squished into a little metallic convertible cube.

She couldn't do it! Could she?

As they had agreed, the kids went out with their friends that evening. In the spirit of their new adult relationship, Stacey didn't ask where they were going, with whom, nor when they would be home. She didn't even remind them of their curfew, although she had to bite her tongue to suppress the habit.

She simply called out "Have a nice evening," as each one left, then settled in with a good book and a glass of red wine. She was reading Borges and, somehow, a rioja felt like the right choice. She wondered if anyone had worked out a guide of wine and literature pairings? Just like those guides which tell you what wine to drink with this or that food, some wines being better for tapas-like nibbles, others best with dessert, maybe some wines brought out the best in Dostoyevsky while others were better consumed while reading Vonnegut?

Stacey pondered that for a moment, took a sip from her glass, read a few paragraphs, took another sip, started a mental list of wine-author pairings, then took another sip. At one point, she decided to go to bed, wondering if it was bad parenting not to wait up until the kids came home or was it showing them that she trusted them? This change in the dynamic of their relationship was moving a little fast for her, but maybe that was better.

5

Brunch

THE NEXT MORNING, Stacey again let the kids sleep in. She had taken her novel downstairs and was installed in an armchair in the living room, book in one hand, a steaming *café au lait* in the other, feet up, sunlight streaming into the room. A sigh of satisfaction escaped her. She loved the quiet of mornings, when everything was still and calm, when everything was possible. She remembered when her children were little. Some mornings, she would sneak into their bedrooms and watch them sleep, enjoying the little animal-like noises they made or the way they stirred then settled back into sleep.

Just like a new day brings new possibilities, small children contain so many possibilities. They could grow up to be presidents or astronauts, school teachers or gardeners. Stacey remembered her son's garbage man phase. He adored everything about them: the big noisy truck, the masher thing on the back, the fact that they were allowed to ride standing up on the outside of the truck. Jean was horrified by the idea. When he told the 4-year-old David that he would never allow him to become a garbage man, David had cried. Stacey consoled him, and David, from the safety of his mother's arms, told his father defiantly, "But Daddy. They take away all the yucky stuff. They make everybody's lives better."

Stacey took a sip of her coffee, warmed by the hot beverage and the memory of her little son's generosity. She was about to return to her reading when Laura sailed in, fully dressed in a lovely pale pink frock. The dress had been the source of an argument not too long before. The family had been invited to a wedding and neither parent could bear the idea of showing up with Laura in one of her black and red accoutrements, so Stacey had gone out and bought the pink dress. The color suited Laura and the cut was just right to show off her slim figure. She looked very pretty in that dress and yet, when Stacey had given it to her, Laura had yelled things about her parents always wanting to control her, that it was a free world, she had a right to choose her own clothes. Here she was, voluntarily wearing that same dress, hair skillfully blown and styled, make-up discreetly applied. Instead of the harsh black liner and blood red lipstick, she had chosen a palette of beiges and browns for her eyes, and a nude gloss for her lips.

"Did you use my make-up?" Stacey asked.

"I'm sorry, Mom," answered Laura. "I should have asked first."

"Yes, you should have," Stacey agreed, before changing the subject. "You look beautiful. Really, really stunning." Laura blushed with pride.

Just then, David walked in, wearing a jacket, slacks and dress shirt, and holding one of his father's ties up to his throat. Skipping the usual good mornings, he jumped right to "What do you guys think? Tie or no tie?"

"Tie," replied Laura, at the same time as Stacey answered "No tie." They all laughed, then Stacey repeated "No tie."

As David turned to put the tie away, Laura asked "Hey David, would you mind if I did something to your hair? There's something...." David cut her off right away.

And the arguing starts, thought Stacey, before

discovering that teenage kids, too, could be full of possibilities.

"I was hoping you would help me," David said to his sister. As they started to leave the living room, discussing whether gel or the blow dryer would help, David called out to Stacey, "You'd better get a move on. We need to leave in fifteen minutes."

Stacey had to laugh at the role reversal but did, indeed, get a move on since she hadn't even showered. A few minutes later, she had showered, dressed in the first dress she had purchased from Corinne and styled her hair the way Annie had shown her. She was in the process of applying her make-up like Françoise had taught her when Laura came in. She watched her mother for a minute or two then offered a few suggestions, a little heavier with that brown on the corner of her eyelid, a slightly different color of blush on the cheeks.... Stacey followed some of the ideas, Laura took the brush out of her hands and applied some make-up herself, and they chatted amicably, like equals—or girlfriends—Stacey enjoying this change from the usual adolescent confrontation.

Suddenly, David ducked his head in, exasperated "It's been twenty minutes. We gotta go!"

"What's the rush?" complained Stacey.

"We don't want to miss the train," replied David.

"So we'll drive."

"No," answered David, firmly. "Laura really wants to reduce our carbon footprint. And I checked out the prices on the web site. The bill is already going to be hefty. If we can save the price of parking..." he trailed off, leaving Stacey bemused. Her techie son taking other people's needs into account! People, not machines.

She hurried to get her jacket and purse and follow the kids out the door to the train station. Only once they were in the train on their way to Paris could she take a moment to ponder the changes in Laura and David and in their relationship with her and with one another. Maybe they were just being nice since they wanted the fancy meal?

She closed her eyes and half-dozed, half-contemplated the question until Laura gently tapped her arm and said, "Time to change trains."

They changed trains then got off at *Charles de Gaule – Etoile*, a huge metro station where the RER A and three metro lines converged. Stacey hated this station because there were many, many exits. Choose the wrong one and you were in for quite a hike. She shouldn't have worried, though; when David had researched the prices, he had also researched how to get there. He gently directly his mother and sister to the *Hoche* exit. They walked up the stairs and emerged into the brilliant sunshine.

L'Etoile was a giant roundabout at the western end of the *Champs-Elysées*, a huge disk with the *Arc de Triomphe* in the middle. Twelve different streets radiated out from the central disk which made driving through it a nightmare, cars coming at you seemingly from all directions. Who had the right of way? There was the legal answer: the car on the right has priority. There was also the practical answer: the car that was the most banged up or had the most aggressive driver. *A lot like life*, thought Stacey.

David had chosen the correct exit. They found themselves on the corner where the *Avenue Hoche* meets *l'Etoile*. They stood there for a few minutes, Stacey watching the traffic patterns. Laura, however, seemed more interested in the touristic side of things, pointing out the Big Bus tour with all the people—and all their cameras—on the open-roof second level of the bus. She squealed with excitement at the *Bustronome*, a bus in which you could have a four course meal prepared by a gourmet chef and see the sights of Paris at the same time. She pointed out Chinese tourists, Indians, Latinos, some Americans. It was very international but one factor united them all: the selfie. Some were cautious and took their selfies with the *Arc de Triomphe* from the sidewalk. Others ventured into traffic, risking life and limb to get a better shot.

While Laura commented on the tourists, David announced the luxury cars: Jaguar, Porsche, Mercedes, Ferrari, old Jag. Stacey smiled at the precision. An Old Jaguar got an entirely different category from a recent model? Suddenly, there was a surge of emotion in David's voice as a car zoomed down the *Avenue Hoche,* making the engine roar.

"Maserati," he said, almost religiously.

It wasn't a coincidence there were so many tourists and so many luxury cars; they were in *les beaux quartiers,* the posh neighborhoods a stone's throw from the Belgian, Qatari and Kazak embassies, near the headquarters for *Lagardère, Cap Gemini* and other multinationals. After a few minutes, Stacey turned to leave. "We really should go," she said. The kids started to follow then stopped in front of a group of electric scooters.

The scooters were a thing from childhood, a base that looked like a skateboard with two wheels, a vertical bar on one side ending in handlebars. You hold the handlebars with both hands, put one foot on the skateboard-y part, then push with the other foot. That was when you were kids. These scooters were equipped with a small electric motor, making them a viable means of transportation in a city known for its traffic jams.

"Can we go for a ride first?" asked Laura, excitedly.

"I can get the app so we can rent them," added David, equally enthused.

Stacey was—well, horrified was probably too strong a word but not by much. Here she was, in her nice dress and heels, and the kids wanted to ride a scooter? She hadn't ridden one of those things in... she started to count backward. It had been at least four decades, maybe four and a half. Not years, decades! And in this neighborhood? What would she look like? What would people think? She wouldn't dare. The thoughts raced through her brain but outwardly she didn't say anything.

Laura noticed her mother's lack of reaction and said, somewhat dejectedly, "No, we should just go to the restaurant."

The trio walked down the street, Stacey a little sad that she had dampened the mood. The young were resilient, however. Soon, they were making jokes about the entrance to an underground parking lot, which looked an awful lot like those public toilet *cabines*, inventing stories about needing a restroom and ending up in the parking lot and vice versa, each story more outlandish than the previous one.

Just as the stories were at their worst, and the kids' laughter at its height, Stacey stopped. She pointed across the road to a large Hausmannian façade, stonework punctuated by large windows, a black awning jutting out above the entrance bedecked by a discreet gilded "RM."

"There," she said.

They crossed the street, passed through a revolving door and entered the dimly lit lobby. Everything was luxurious: the plush, padded carpet, the round mahogany table facing the door, the immense bouquet, about the same size as the table, handing upside down above it.

Stacey, Laura and David crossed the lobby to the maître d's desk. "*Bonjour,*" said Stacey. "We would like brunch, please."

"Do you have a reservation?" inquired the maître d'.

"No," replied Stacey, suddenly worried that her outing was going to fall flat. "Is that a problem?"

"Not at all. You just won't be able to sit in the courtyard. Please follow me."

He led Stacey and her kids to a round table near a window which opened up on the courtyard where they could see other diners already eating. The maître d' held the chair for Stacey, then motioned to Laura and held the chair for her as well. As he left, David sat down, trying to hold back his laughter. Laura caught his eye and burst out laughing too, then checked herself and took it down to a discreet chuckle, more fitting with the setting.

"I've never had anyone hold the chair for me before," she said.

David chuckled back. "I know. Right?"

Before Laura could answer, a waitress approached their table. "Hello, I'm Marie. I'll be taking care of you today. Can I get you started with a cocktail?"

The kids looked hopefully at their mother. "No, thank you," she said, knowing that this would not be included in the already outrageous price of the prix-fixe buffet. "Perhaps a coffee?"

"Coffee? Espresso? *Noisette*? *Café au lait*?" Stacey nodded. "Tea ? Hot chocolate? We also have fresh juices." She started to recite a long list of drinks, from the mundane apple or orange juice to three berry or orange-banana-carrot or even more exotic combinations.

David couldn't stand it any longer. He broke in with his order. Marie nodded, then asked Laura what she would like.

"Well, I'd like my brother to be a little more polite to you," Laura said. The young waitress smiled but didn't say anything, always discreet as befits a *Palace*. "As far as drinks go, a triple berry juice, please."

Again, Marie nodded. "Please help yourself to the buffet. Your drinks will be here when you return." She backed away from the table before turning and heading away. The kids got up and walked over to the buffet, Stacey on their heels.

At first glance, the buffet was a little disappointing. Given that her friends had said brunch here was "*géant!*" she was expecting something, well, bigger. There were only four long tables. By American standards... as she looked at the contents of those four tables, Stacey stopped herself mid-thought. The size might be small by American standards but the contents were off the charts. On the closest counter, clearly targeting children, a chocolate fountain flanked by an assortment of cut fruit on one side and bowls of candy on the other. The second table held a variety of breads, French and international breakfast pastries, a platter of Pierre Hermé macarons and six different choices of single serving cakes. The third table was the most densely stocked. French cheeses shared the limelight with Lebanese mezze, the tabbouleh segueing into other vegetable salads, then *charcuterie*, *terrines*, and lox, which made for a natural transition to sushi. The farthest table, where Stacey headed first, contained hot food, with wait staff behind the counter ready to serve the patrons.

Stacey found the plates, handed one to each of her kids, took one for herself and went to the far end of the "hot" counter. She chose a little of this, a little of that.

She opened one warming plate, couldn't identify the contents and so asked the waitress.

"Oh, that's black cod poached in miso. It's really good."

Stacey had learned long ago the wisdom of listening to the wait staff. After all, they were the only people to taste the entire menu, not just one dish. She took a few small pieces of the fish, along with some zucchini from the neighboring dish, which seemed to please the young woman.

"If I may," she continued, pointing to something in the first dish. "That's *confit* of eggplant. I think you'll like it."

Stacey thanked her as she put two pieces of miso-confit eggplant on her plate next to the fish, much to the young woman's approval. She finished choosing her first round then returned to the table, just as Laura and David arrived back as well, their drinks waiting for them just as Marie had promised.

"Wow!" exclaimed Laura, as she sat down.

"I know," David added. "Everything looks amazing."

"I don't think amazing is strong enough," replied Laura, cutting a small piece of her *aumonière*.

"Over-amazing?" asked David, taking a forkful of caramelized beef.

For two full minutes, there was silence at their table as each one chewed, slowly, then more slowly, savoring the intense flavors, a look of pure enjoyment on their faces. When at the table, silence was probably the highest compliment a Frenchman could give the chef. Silence meant the food was so good that one had to stop all other distractions, even conversation, in order to concentrate fully on it, to mobilize one's senses completely in order to do the cuisine justice. It was almost a spiritual moment, a rapture.

Finally, Laura swallowed. "Oh my God!" she exclaimed.

"*C'est géant!*" David added.

Stacey smiled to herself. Exactly what her friends had meant. "What is that?" she asked Laura.

"It's an *aumonière*," Laura answered. "It's got duck *confit*, but there's something else." She took another bite and closed her eyes, trying to identify the other ingredient. "It's really frustrating. I know that flavor, but what is it? It's on the tip of my tongue."

"Literally," joked David.

Laura laughed, then put a small piece on both her mom's and David's plate. "Here. Tell me what you think." David tasted the morsel Laura had given him.

He chewed slowly, the concentration on his face

giving way to puzzlement. "Fruity. Sweet but not too sweet," he pronounced. "You're right. It's like I've always known this flavor yet it's not something we eat often. It's not an everyday flavor." Laura nodded in agreement.

Stacey tasted her piece and smiled. She knew why the kids found this flavor so familiar. "Quince jam," she stated.

"Of course!" cried David.

"Like *Mamie* used to make!" Laura exclaimed. She and David started talking about all the jams their grandmother used to make, then all the *crêpes* with homemade jam she would prepare for their afternoon snack, which naturally led the conversation to her cakes and pastries. "Remember when she made that *forêt noire* for Christmas?" asked Laura.

David nodded. "Best Christmas ever," he added as he finished off the last tidbit on his plate.

That was something else the French did. When a meal was very good, there was often silence. Then, after the first wave of appreciation passed, they would start to discuss other great meals. If the conversation progressed to holidays or weddings, the hostess would know that her meal was world class. When she had first come to France, Stacey had found this behavior strange and off-putting; now, she took it for what it was—a compliment. Her kids were showing their appreciation for this fine brunch.

David looked at his empty plate then over at his mom's and sister's. "You guys ready to go back?" They were, so they all got up and walked to the buffet, each one attracted to something a little different. When they came back to the table, the empty plates had been cleared, fresh silverware set out, and their napkins expertly refolded and set to the left of their forks.

"Like Dobby the house elf," snickered David.

New beverages awaited them, too; fruit juice for the kids, a *café au lait* for Stacey. Stacey stared for a few minutes at the cup and saucer.

"What's wrong, Mom?" asked Laura.

"Nothing's wrong," Stacey answered. "It's just not the same cup as before."

"That's normal. You get a clean one each time."

Stacey laughed. "That's not what I meant." The cup was white porcelain with the outside decorated in a shiny metallic silver finish. The white saucer had a black and white design on one spot. Looking at the saucer, it appeared to be an ink blot and nothing more. When Stacey looked at the ink blot in the reflection of the cup, however, she saw a human eye. She turned the cup and saucer around so her kids could see.

"Woah! That is so cool!" they both exclaimed, almost simultaneously, looked at each other surprised, then laughed. Stacey hadn't seen such camaraderie between the two of them since they were little.

The meal progressed in a similar manner: they would chat— about the food, about the other diners, about the beautiful modern "design elements of the space" as Laura called it. They would get up for another serving and come back to newly folded napkins and another design on Stacey's coffee cup—an eye, red lips, a pink ring, a blue butterfly. And then chat about that, too. It was natural, it was relaxed, and it was everything Stacey had always dreamed family life could be.

This is wonderful, even though Jean isn't here, Stacey thought, before a doubt crept into her mind. Or maybe it's wonderful because Jean isn't here.

6

One singular sensation

AT ONE POINT Stacey stopped going back to the buffet, despite not having tasted everything. Then Laura stopped, and a serving or two later, David sat back in his chair and said "*Je n'en peux plus.*" I can't take any more.

"I should hope so," answered Laura, her natural snark returning. "You had two or three of everything."

Ordinarily, that would have been enough to start a fight between the two of them. Today, though, David just chuckled and said, "I wanted to make sure Mom got her money's worth."

Laura laughed, then replied something which made the two of them laugh more. They continued chatting together while Stacey paid the bill and left a nice tip for Marie who, despite it being a buffet, had been a very attentive waitress.

Since they had trained in, that meant training home so Stacey, always the mother, suggested that they go to the restroom before leaving. Usually in France, one goes to *les toilettes*. At the Royal Monceau, however, 'restroom' was a more appropriate term because the facilities were so large, each one almost a room in and of itself, and they are so calm and so large you could, actually, take a nap. Each "stall" (for want of a better word) had the floor and four walls covered in marble. One end of the space contained the toilet; on the other end a mirror in a shiny chrome frame hanging above a chrome vanity holding the sink, towels, Kleenex, soap and hand creams. What had David had said earlier? "Over amazing." It just about summed up the toilets, too.

The restrooms were upstairs, so Stacey waited for her kids on the landing before walking back down the stairs. Not just any stairs. The crazily luxurious, over the top décor continued here, too. A dozen chandeliers were suspended midway from the ceiling by swathes of white silk, each lightbulb covered in a tiny white lampshade, swags of crystal beads dangling between the branches of the chandeliers. It was dazzling, even more so since the walls of the stairwell, covered in floor to ceiling mirrors, reflected and multiplied the chandeliers, making you feel they carried on forever.

The result was, Stacey felt, enchanting.

David, too, was under its charm. "It's just like Hogwarts," he said as he walked down the stairs with his mom.

Laura stayed at the top. When her mother and brother were halfway down, she started sidestepping down the stairs, one by one, singing just loud enough so they could hear, "One," a step, "singular sensation," step close step," every little step she takes," and a series of steps. Stacey, caught by surprise, said nothing, but David, quicker-witted, sang "da da da da da da" as his sister continued her imitation of *A Chorus Line*.

As they left the establishment, walked back to the metro station and trained home, they relived their brunch experience, re-discussed this or that dish, mimicked the maître d' or Laura's surprise at having the chair held for her, and generally had as much fun going home as they had had at the restaurant itself. When they neared their train stop, Stacey glanced at her watch and only then realized how late it was.

"It's almost five," she informed her kids.

"So what?" answered David.

"We spent almost four hours at brunch," Stacey continued. "You're not going to have a lot of time for your friends."

"Four hours!" exclaimed Laura. "Is that a world record?"

"Definitely a personal best," replied David, patting his stomach. The kids' joking continued in that vein, not a word about missing out on time with friends nor a complaint about their mom's outing taking so long, just enjoyment at having spent this time together.

7

The end of the weekend

ONCE HOME, however, Laura quickly changed clothes and went to a friend's house, David did something on his computer, and all three generally went about their business until dinner when, almost magically, the kids appeared once again to help out. Earlier in the weekend, Stacey was tempted to think they were helping simply because they wanted their outings. Mercenaries. Now, Sunday evening, they had nothing to gain. It was kindness, pure and simple.

Just as dinner was ready, Jean arrived home. It was

annoying seeing him there, seemingly happy with his weekend. They all sat down together at the table, Jean surprised to discover that the meal was only a light vegetable broth, and even more surprised to learn that the kids were just fine with this.

"What's going on?" he asked. "Why aren't we having a proper meal?"

Before Stacey could reply, David said, "I'm still so full from brunch. A bowl of soup is more than enough."

"Oh I know," Laura agreed. "I keep thinking about the caramelized beef."

"And the *aumonière*," added David.

The kids relived the brunch once again, telling their father in detail about the food and also the "*Monceau* experience" as Laura called it. When Jean complained again about just having soup for dinner, Laura answered, "It is *homemade* soup, you know. Do you realize how long it takes to make?"

David added "If you want something more, you can always get up and look in the fridge for yourself. You know where it is, right?"

Stacey had to laugh, albeit inwardly. Nothing like two teenagers to put you in your place.

The kids were in a great mood, laughing and joking, visibly pleased by their weekend experiences. And Jean?

Stacey couldn't tell. Little by little, though, the kids' good humor rubbed off on him. He relaxed and started asking questions about their weekend.

Stacey looked around the table, at Laura, David and Jean, enjoying this moment of harmony. Just then, Laura's phone buzzed.

Laura took the phone out and looked at the message. She tapped on the photo someone had sent and enlarged it with her fingers. She inspected every nook and cranny of the photo, getting more and more upset.

"What's wrong, dear?" Stacey asked.

"It's Michel," she answered.

Ah, her boyfriend, Stacey thought.

"Look," she said as she flashed her phone to them all. "I can't believe it!"

She started to cry then stood up and ran upstairs to her room, muttering, "I can't believe it," the whole way.

"I didn't see the photo," Stacey said, perplexed.

"Me neither," Jean said.

"I did," said David. "Michel kissing Vanessa. At a party. Must've been Friday when we went out together. He's such a douche. He's already got the prettiest girl in school and he has to go kiss that slut?"

Stacey felt a pang. David defending his sister.

"Her boyfriend kissed another girl?" Jean got up, too,

and started pacing. "How dare that little punk. I'll have no daughter of mine treated this way! I'll ..." and he continued, with a long, long list of what Stacey hoped were empty threats.

"I'd better go talk with her," Stacey said, rising from the table. "David, can you clear the dishes? There's a cake in the fridge. Maybe see if your dad wants some."

David looked over at his father who was still pacing, still fuming.

"Don't worry, Mom. I'll take care of things here," he said as he reached to gather the plates.

Stacey walked upstairs. Her friends had said adultery was no longer accepted in France, and here was Jean, proving them right, angry that someone was cheating on Laura. Maybe that was the true test: if it's not OK for your kids. And what did that mean? It's OK for Stacey to be treated this way but not OK for Laura? Was she worth so little in his eyes?

Stacey knocked on the closed door.

"Can I come in?" she called. Through the door, she could hear Laura sobbing.

"Yes," Laura said.

Stacey went in. Her daughter was lying on her bed, crying. Stacey sat down next to her and put her arm around her.

"I'm so sorry," she said.

"Not your fault," Laura managed to say between sobs. "It's me. I'm not good enough." She broke off, crying harder.

"Look at you," Stacey said, her tone sharper than she meant. Laura stopped sobbing for a moment, surprised. "You're beautiful. Even David said you're the prettiest girl in school and Michel is a douche."

Laura smiled. "He did?"

"He did."

"No one says 'douche' anymore," said Laura, wiping her nose on her sleeve, just like she did when she was a little girl. Stacey winced, stifling the urge to give her daughter a tissue. Instead, she gave her a hug.

"You're beautiful. You're smart. You're passionate about art." Laura nodded, sniffling. "You're a fabulous young woman and you deserve someone who thinks highly of you and treats you well."

As the words came out of her mouth, Stacey thought that she, too, was beautiful. She, too, was smart.

"If Michel kissed another girl," she continued, "then maybe he's the one who's not good enough." Again, Stacey's thoughts turned to her relationship with Jean.

Laura's sobbing had stopped and her sniffling started to slow at the same time as, inwardly, Stacey's sobbing began. She just realized why she had been lashing out, doing all those stupid, ineffectual revenge schemes. Because she felt hurt. She had felt, just like Laura now. She had devoted her life to this man, and he made her feel that she wasn't good enough.

Stacey turned her attention back to Laura, who was calmer now.

"You know what they say, right? *Mieux vaut être seul que mal accompagné.*" Better off alone than in bad company.

Laura sniffed.

"Besides," Stacey continued, "you won't be alone for long. David says there are at least ten guys at school who want to go out with you."

"He did?" Laura asked.

"He did," Stacey answered, giving Laura's hand a little squeeze. "So take a little time and choose one who will treat you right."

Laura wiped her eyes and hugged her mother. "You're right. *I'm* gonna choose."

"There's some cake downstairs. You want some?"

Laura got up to go, then stopped, looking at her mom who was still sitting on her bed.

"Mom, you coming?"

"I'll be right down," Stacey answered.

Laura headed downstairs.

The storms of youth pass quickly, thought Stacey. Hers, well. She sighed. Everything she had told Laura was true. She did deserve a man who treated her well. She should choose right... But a marriage was different from a high school flirt. There were the kids, the house, all those years together. You didn't just throw them away...

Stacey got up and walked slowly downstairs, more unsure than ever.

Part III

"Dans la vie, il ne faut compter que sur soi-même, et encore pas beaucoup."
- Alphonse Allais

In life, you can only count on yourself--
and even then, maybe not.

1

Luxemburg gardens

BY THE END of the week, Laura's boyfriend had become no more than a distant memory. Stacey felt drained. She had been the supportive mom all week, despite feeling confused and hurt by Jean's double standard. How could he criticize the boyfriend for something that he, Jean, was guilty of? She just couldn't make sense of it.

Stacey was feeling burned out and she deserved a treat, so she made plans to meet her friend Evelyne in Paris for lunch and shopping.

She trained in to the city and had just arrived when her phone rang. It was Evelyne.

"Oh Stacey, I'm so sorry. I have to cancel," Evelyne said. Stacey could hear water running in the background.

"Is anything wrong?" It wasn't like Evelyne to cancel.

"Everything is wrong. The washing machine started to overflow so I tried to turn off the intake valve and it broke. I've got water everywhere."

"Do you need some help?" Stacey asked. "Do you want me to come?"

"No, don't worry," Evelyne answered. "The plumber should be here any minute. I'm just so sorry..." she trailed off.

"It's normal," Stacey said. "You take care of that and we'll have lunch another time." She forced a cheery tone, despite feeling disappointed. Lunch with Evelyne was supposed to be her reward, time off for good behavior...

Yet, here she was. In Paris, on a beautiful day. Even though she was alone, it would be a shame to waste such a beautiful day.

What to do? she thought.

Before she could decide, she turned the corner and saw a Starbucks. Nothing better for treating herself. She went in, bought a slice of carrot cake and a chai tea venti, feeling a little pleased with herself for having exact change.

She munched and sipped her way down the boulevard Montparnasse.

Since she was so close to the Luxembourg Gardens, she'd visit the garden and decide what to do afterward. As she walked, she spotted an ATM machine and decided she'd better get some cash. Starbucks had cleaned her out, and it was always good to have a little cash in case of emergencies. She got two crisp fifty Euro bills which she put away, with her credit card, in her wallet before continuing down the boulevard Montparnasse to where it crossed the boulevard Saint Michel and entered the gardens through its southern tip.

She loved the Luxembourg Gardens. It was one of the rare places in which her American soul slowed down enough to do what the French call *flâner*. It was ironic that this was a verb, an action, when the point of *flâner* was to do as little as possible. Deadlines and goals had no purpose here. Time did not exist. To properly "do" the Luxembourg Gardens, you had to sit down in one of those green metal chairs, if you found one free, and bask in the sun. Or people watch. Or, multi-tasking *à la française*, sunbathe and people watch at the same time. For hours. No one would disturb you, no one would hurry you, except, of course, for the guardian at the end of the day when he closed the park for the night. The best spot to hang out was near the pond in front of the Senate building. On a fine day like today, there would be children sailing their little boats in the water and the inevitable drama when one of the boats lost the breeze and stopped in the middle of the water, the child cried and the parents argued with the man who rented the boats over who should wade in to retrieve it. One of those universal human dramas that played out generation after generation, yet the parents, who had surely cried over a lost boat as children themselves, continued to rent the little boats for their own kids.

She would go sit there later. First, she wandered through the small orchard. The trees, behind bars to protect them from the visitors, looked like they were in jail, each one pruned and tortured into a precise geometric shape. Later in the season, each fruit would be neatly tucked into its own little paper bag to protect it from insects. The oh-so-cartesian French had a way of whipping nature into shape, making it follow mathematical principals instead of letting it be natural and wild. That was for the *jardins à l'anglaise*, which she found funny since the British and their stiff upper lips were far from natural and wild.

She passed by a large grass field, bordered by flowers and trees, then headed toward the beehives (she had read once there were one million bees lodged here), to listen to the hubbub of the miniature bee city. As she strolled, she started feeling the consequences of that chai tea latte more and more, so headed toward the pay-for-play swing sets and the adjoining snack counter. There was a public restroom attached to it. She was about to order something to eat (in France, "pay-for-play" applies to public restrooms, too) when she saw a small sign in the window: *WC hors service*. Restroom out of order.

"No worry," she reassured herself. There were more restrooms a bit further on. She continued on, no longer strolling and loitering but walking with a purpose. She passed the tennis courts and then, to the left, there it was, a small green wooden building. She entered, stopped at the sign "toilettes: 0,50€" and got out her wallet. Damn! No coins in the coin purse. She had used all her change at Starbucks. She flicked through the bills. Only two, the fifties she had withdrawn earlier that morning. She knew this wasn't going to work, but the drink she had drunk was more insistent than ever.

She offered one of the bills to the restroom attendant and asked, meekly, "Can you make change?"

The answer was brutal. And long. Far too long for someone with a chai tea venti—or a venti anything for that matter—in her bladder.

"What if you keep 10€ and return 40?" her tone

desperate. Madame Pipi, keeping rule and order in her realm, would not be bribed.

Stacey understood but couldn't wait for the end of the sermon. She fled, tucking the two bills into her front pocket, hastily crossing the park, barely glimpsing at the pond, the sailboats, the children, the people watchers. She turned the corner of the Senate building, no time to admire the beautifully groomed flowerbed on the left or the Medicis fountain on the right. Out the gate, across the street to the Odeon Theatre, desperately looking for a café or someplace where she could use the ladies' room. Without being yelled at.

It was not her lucky day.

One café was closed for the day, its chairs stacked up and chained together on the miniscule terrace. Another café was closed for remodeling. A long line of tourists over there. Art gallery, bookstore, boutique hotel, another bookstore? An overabundance of culture yet a dearth of toilets! She kept going, the situation more critical with each step, cursing herself all the way for ordering a 'venti' instead of a 'grande'. She wouldn't have to go so badly, and she would have had change left for Madame Pipi. Shoulda, coulda, woulda. She passed a restaurant, closed after the lunch service, "Le Schmuck," and had to giggle. That was Jean—*le schmuck*. A few streets further on, as her desperation reached its apex, she spotted a store front that looked like someone had boarded up the windows. A small spotlight highlighted a menu against the paneling. Someone pushed the bright blue door and walked in.

In! It was open!

Whatever it was, it was open. She walked in and was amazed. The same wood paneling as outside, low lighting, a massive long bar with a barman working away, preparing a cocktail. He looked up when she walked in.

She mouthed the words "Les toilettes, s'il vous plait."

With a nod of his head, he indicated the direction. No questions, no lecturing. What a relief!

A few minutes later, when the relief was complete, she made her way back to the bar and sat down on one of the stools. The barman placed a menu in front of her with a warm smile.

2

Bum in a bar

AFTERWARD, WHEN Stacey thought back through the chain of events, she wondered just how she had started talking with the man sitting next to her at the bar. Did she, so relieved by finally finding the ladies' room, let down her guard and say something to him? Or did he strike up a conversation, knowing from long experience how to wheedle his way into free drinks? She didn't know.

Partway through the cocktail she had ordered, she found herself talking to this person. He was normally dressed, clean shaven, clean. Really, he looked just like anyone else, only little by little, as the small talk progressed did she realize he was out of work. And homeless. It was all kind of random, when she thought about it.

As was what came next.

"The trouble with you," he began, studying her blurrily over the edge of his glass.

Oh no, she thought. *Yet another 'the trouble with you' conversation.* She had them with her husband all the time. Or, rather, he had them with her and she merely submitted to the exercise. It was some sort of mansplaining thing... although, now that she thought about it, her mother did that, too. Maybe that was why she let other people have opinions about who she was and tell her what was wrong with her. Well, she would do that no longer. She had come here for the ladies' room, not for a therapy session. She would put an end to this conversation right now.

Right as Stacey opened her mouth to interrupt this know-it-all, he said something truly disturbing.

"Your problem," he began again, "is that you stopped living your own life."

Stacey closed her mouth, flustered by his words.

"You loved your husband," the man carried on, "you wanted to make him happy, so you started doing things to please him. Make his favorite meals. Wear dresses in his favorite colors. Then you had kids and loved them, too. Maybe the girl doesn't like broccoli, so you stopped making it. Maybe your boy can't bear classical music, so you stopped going to concerts and switched to football games instead. What about your friends? One's an alcoholic so the group stopped the evenings out in a pub. I bet you even got stuck preparing the dinner parties." He chuckled into his drink.

Stacey was dumbstruck. It was true. Maybe not the details, but it was true all the same. She had stopped doing a lot of things she liked to do in order to accommodate her family, taking less space so that they could take more.

Was that wrong? she wondered. Isn't that what you do for people you love? You take care of them...

He continued, implacable. "Little by little, their likes, dislikes, needs and desires took up more and more space in your life, pushing out any time or energy for your own. You make their lives better, but you forgot about living yours.

"So what are you afraid of? If you stop making everybody happy, the world will fall apart? They'll leave you? You'll lose everything? Sorry to tell you, but you've already lost. You're worried about losing your house, your fancy clothes, your credit card which buys me drinks." He lifted his empty class inquiringly.

Confused, unable to end this conversation but not wanting for it to continue, Stacey gestured to the bartender for another round for them both.

"In the morning, I never know if I'll sleep that night in a bed or on the street, but every morning I can choose to do exactly what I want. I don't have any of the fine things that you have, but I have my freedom, my choices, my dreams, my life."

The bartender placed a full glass in front of each of them. The bum took his, raised it to her in a toast, saying "The way I see it, I've got more than you, lady." He downed the whiskey as if it were a shot of cheap tequila, and wiped his mouth with the back of his hand.

His words hit home, pummeling her like a boxer's blows.

3

Aftermath

I N A D A Z E, Stacey paid the barman, picked up her handbag and left without a word to her drinking partner, who was still talking, swirling the ice cubes in the bottom of the whiskey glass, eyeing the full glass she was abandoning, happy to have a little more alcohol in his future.

Could he be right? Was the problem really her and not her no-good cheating schmuck of a husband? Or that totty? Was she, Stacey, really the problem?

She felt as if the wind had been knocked out of her,

like she had received one blow too many, punch drunk. The image of the demolition scene she had seen on the train that one day flashed in front of her eyes. The heavy ball on the long chain slowly swung backward, away from the building and then, at the end of its arc, changed directions and moved toward the building, inexorably, picking up speed as it moved closer and closer, crashing into the wall, tearing apart side wall, glass, doors. Again and again, gutting the building until floors crashed into one another, leaving just the façade and enough of the supporting walls to keep it upright. Jean's trysts, the bum's words, had gutted her like that building until only a shell remained, a façade that looked fine from the street but held only emptiness.

She leaned against a wall for support, head reeling, trying to breathe deeply to stop all the metaphors from swarming around in her brain, closing her eyes with the effort. Just as her mind began to clear, her phone rang. The kids had both said they would stay over with friends that night, so it wouldn't be them. She looked at the caller: Jean. She slipped the phone back in her handbag and started walking again. More steadily.

Was she an empty shell? Walking, thinking. Who was she, anyway? Thinking, walking, reflecting on identity, who she had been way back when, who she had become, how much of her identity was based on her relationships with others, the mother of, the wife of, the daughter of, the friend of. How many of her actions were based on the likes and dislikes of other people?

It suddenly seemed all of Paris was conspiring to answer these questions. Across the street was a storefront from the 1920's called "To the good mother." In a bookstore window, the economic treatise *Starting Over, why the last decade was so damn rotten and why the next one will surely be better.* Next to *Madam Bovary.* Next to a quote from Tennessee Williams printed poster size,

"A prayer for the wild at heart,

Kept in cages."

What a crazy combination! she thought. No one in their right mind would put these together and think it was good marketing. It must mean something.

A car passed by, the radio blaring Destiny's Child's "I'm a Survivor."

It was exactly what she needed to hear at exactly the right moment. *It can't be a coincidence...* It was as if the universe were trying to tell her something. But what?

Pondering, musing, she walked some more and saw a blackboard easel in front of a café: "A hug in every mug! Disclaimer: actual hug sold separately and may vary based on barista's willingness." She could use a hug right now.

She sneaked a look at the barista. Maybe she didn't need a hug quite that much.

Her phone rang again. Jean again. Her thoughts were still too confused to talk with anyone, let alone him. The phone stopped ringing and she put it away, just in time to hear the beep-beep signaling that he left a message.

Stacey crossed the street, a wide avenue with a traffic island in the middle, forcing pedestrians to cross halfway, wait for a light, then cross the rest of the way. A long air vent extended out toward the intersection. Someone had tied long red and orange ribbons on the metal grid. The ribbons danced and swayed with the hot air rising from the metro below, a multicolored ballet which no one else seemed to notice. It was beautiful, yet she was the only one to notice, everyone else too busy or too important to remark.

Stacey spent a few moments enjoying this poetic sight, then continued walking, a quieter neighborhood now, smaller streets. In a shop window—was it a shop? or more of a yoga studio-- hung a lovely hand-painted poster, brightly colored malas decoratively spaced with, in the middle, "What if you take one step each month for your well-being?" She thought about that. Did she do things to take care of herself? All these years, she took care of the kids. That's normal. She took care of Jean. Maybe she shouldn't have. Or not so much. If she had taken as much care of herself as she did of him, would things be different now?

As she turned the street corner, this new line of thought followed her. All the way to the Seine, then along the quays. Looking over at the Pont Alexandre III, she saw a wedding party: bride, groom, maid of honor, best man, taking photos with the Parisian monuments in the background. She stopped to watch as the bride struck a pose, the full, frothy skirt ending in a long train, tight bodice showing off her slim waist and delicate shoulders. She held her bouquet almost as an afterthought. The bride was beautiful. Young. Deliriously happy. Princess for a day. The photographer snapped off a dozen photos or so, then motioned to the groom who stepped into the photo, an arm automatically encircling the waist of his beloved in a gesture both proprietary and comfortable. A few photos looking at the camera then he leaned in to kiss his bride, too happy to wait.

She remembered her wedding day. They, too, had been young and beautiful, just like this couple. She saw Jean again in his tuxedo. He was so handsome that day, a little shy next to her in her glamorous gown. She remembered feeling so lucky to be loved like that and to love him so much. To love and to be loved really was a gift from the gods, which somehow we forgot or grew accustomed to and took for granted over the years.

She took another look at the scene, the maid of honor and best man in the photo now, in sometimes serious, sometimes comical poses. She silently wished them well and continued down the Seine, remembering her wedding, those early years, how poor they had been, how happy they had been.

Her phone rang yet again, interrupting her daydreaming. Caller ID showed her husband's number. Again.

She knew the kids were fine. They both had plans to spend the night at a friend's house. If Jean kept calling like this, it was because he wanted her to do something for him. Or to give her another of his excuses for coming home late. She wasn't in the mood for either.

She didn't answer before so he was going to keep calling, like a two-year-old tugging at his mommy's skirt until she gives in? The phone rang, went to voice mail, rang again, stopped. As it began ringing a fourth time, a flyer tacked up on a street light caught her eye. It was a photocopied poster for a local *ciné-club* touting their upcoming film festival. The headline in big, bold letters, "Home Sweet Home." The background image: the Bates Motel. Just as she let out a laugh, the phone rang again.

She looked at the poster, looked at Jean's name on the screen, and back at the poster. Life with Jean suddenly felt stifling, pushing her to be someone she wasn't. Had she become the mother? Or Norman Bates?

Her phone rang again. She took aim and threw it into the Seine.

And instantly felt better.

Lighter.

Independent.

She started walking once again, a spring in her step, a click in her heels.

As Maya Angelou wrote, "it's the fire in her eyes, and the flash of her teeth, the swing in her waist, and the joy in her feet." When the phone sank into the Seine, something changed inside her: she stood a little straighter, she swung her hips a little more freely. She felt phenomenal.

Men felt it, too. As she walked on, heads turned, just like in the shopping mall after her make-over with the girls. The difference now was that there was no make-over nor any new clothes. It was just Stacey, dressed as always, but something new sparkled inside her. The French, blasé Parisians that they were, would never swarm like a hive of honey bees, but their eyes certainly followed her as she passed by. Heads turned, too. Literally. Now and then, eyes met, locked for a brief instant, a seductive smile appeared on masculine lips.

All the attention felt good.

Between the outdoor cafés and all the tourists, the sidewalks were crowded. Stacey felt a little like a salmon swimming upstream.

This was another cultural difference between the French and, well, pretty much everyone else. When the French walked on the sidewalk, they took the entire space, two people abreast on a normal sidewalk, five to seven people abreast on large sidewalks such as on the *Champs Elysées*. If someone came from the other direction, too bad. They would keep walking, forcing the other person to step into the gutter. It was just plain rude. After all these years, Stacey still didn't understand how people who were very polite otherwise could have such bad manners on a sidewalk. Now, on this sidewalk, Stacey could immediately separate the tourists from the natives: that young man, walking with his friend, just interrupted his conversation to move behind the friend, letting Stacey pass by, definitely a tourist; that mother, firmly guiding her son to the right of the sidewalk, another tourist (ok, the fact that they were both very tall and blond was a tip-off); those two teenage girls, walking and talking and actually bumping into Stacey! French. It was *so* irritating.

Lost in her thoughts, she barely noticed the first message, a teenage girl with "Hello" blazoned across the chest of her t-shirt. The girl smiled at her kindly, but Stacey didn't really think anything of it.

A few steps further on, another t-shirt "Hello my dear," as if the universe was chiding her for not paying attention the first time. *What a coincidence*, she thought. Two tourists wearing such similar t-shirts walking so close to one another.

Or was it a coincidence?

Not even a block further, another t-shirt declared "Fabulous!" Its wearer, an older woman, looked Stacey directly in the eye and winked exactly at the moment they crossed one another on the sidewalk. Stacey had the distinct impression that the wink, and the message, was meant for her personally.

Then it got weirder.

On a young guy, tall, slim, very metrosexual, the slogan "The future is female." Again, direct eye contact with its wearer.

On a stylish woman about her age. "Every flower blooms in its own time," along with a reassuring smile.

On a thirtysomething man, very virile, built to play rugby, "Think better, think bigger." Had she been thinking too small? Was there more out there for her than her cheating husband?

As if to answer that question, she crossed paths with a woman in her early forties. A truly beautiful woman. Tall, slim, thick chestnut hair falling midway down her back, regular features, piercing blue eyes, walking with a fluid, feline grace. Like the others, this woman looked at Stacey directly in the eyes and smiled warmly for a fraction of a second, as if to say, "Yes, this is for you." On her t-shirt was written, "Inside each woman is a wild thing. Let her out."

Stacey instantly knew it was true.

If she were honest, that is, if she thought better, if she thought bigger, she had always sensed there was something else inside her, something wilder, more fabulous than the wife and mother that she was. Those were both roles she loved, but they seemed to have grown too small these last few years. Ever since their "intervention," David and Laura had shown that they, too, had outgrown their need for a mommy and wanted something different from her.

At fifty, she was still a bud, waiting to bloom.

The t-shirt messages continued. One woman wore a sexy tight black dress emblazoned with "plants not plastics" in white. Stacey scoffed at the irony of this message being worn by someone with more than her fair share of silicone in her body.

On a 20-something man (*boy?* Stacey thought) a dictionary definition, "Mobilophobia: Fear of being without a mobile phone." Stacey laughed at the difference in generations.

These youngsters really were afraid of life without the constant crutch of a mobile phone. It was almost like their security blanket or favorite stuffed toy. Stacey remembered life before the ubiquitous mobile phone; they had gotten along just fine. Heck, she had just thrown her phone into the Seine and felt great. What could possibly go wrong?

The next t-shirt she passed was more somber, "The past is gone." Was it? Was it really? Until a few weeks ago, she had been a happy wife and mother, in love with Jean despite all those years together. Or, perhaps, thanks to all those years, because she had felt her love deepening and maturing over time. Was that all gone? Could it not be recaptured somehow?

Stacey was distracted from these thoughts by yet another t-shirt. Letters so large they barely fit into the t-shirt: "Smile". She did. The handsome man wearing the shirt smiled back, warmly, kindly.

Apophenia, Stacey thought. Apophenia was the perception of meaningful connections where, in fact, there were none. All those t-shirts, signs, posters—it had felt like there was a sense to it all, that the universe was trying to tell her something, something vitally important, something she needed to understand now in order to take action. What if it was only apophenia?

4

Meeting the girls

STACEY CONTINUED walking, lost in her musings, when suddenly she heard someone calling her name and pounding on a window. She turned toward the sound to see the shop girl Corinne run out of a small café, leaving Annie and Françoise inside.

"Stacey! What are you doing here?" called Corinne. Now, that was a good question, with a very long answer. Too much information, as her kids would say. Instead, she replied, "Just doing a little shopping in Paris."

Corinne, noticing the absence of shopping bags, frowned but simply said, "Come join us for a coffee." The girls inside the café were waving excitedly to her, Corinne was gently pushing her, so Stacey went in.

The girls were sharing a pastry with their coffee. It looked like a rectangular piece of apple pie with a lattice-work top crust, instead of the standard open-face tart the French usually prefer. Corinne saw her looking at it. "You want one?" she asked.

"What is it?"

"Une jalousie aux pommes."

Apple jealousy? You can't make this up, Stacey thought. It couldn't be apophenia if even the desserts were mocking her. She repeated silently the t-shirt mantra "Think better, think bigger."

"No, just a *grand crème*, please."

The coffee came accompanied by a little pot of hot milk and several little packets of sugar. As she picked up one of the packets, Stacey noticed the words "Lavazza: Express Yourself." The words were printed both in French and English, as if to drive home the point.

If the universe really is sending me signs, it's becoming a little heavy-handed, she thought.

Stacey followed Lavazza's instructions and started telling the others the recent events of her life, the girls asking questions here, making comments there, generally coaxing all the details out of her. As the story emerged, Corinne, clearly the ring-leader, took charge.

"You need some fun," she said at the very moment that "Girls, they just wanna, they just wanna, girls just wanna have fun," played over the sound system of the café. Annie and Françoise nodded in agreement—with Corinne? Or with Cindy Lauper? Corinne began enumerating different ideas, different plans, ranging from silly to extravagant, the other girls adding comments and ideas now and again, like bank robbers planning their next heist. Stacey looked into her coffee as she stirred it absentmindedly, lost somewhere between the lull of the girls' voices and the froth in the milk.

She came back to herself in time to hear Annie exclaim, "It's decided then," setting her coffee cup back into the saucer with a little bang that made her spoon rattle.

She elbowed Stacey gently to move her out of the booth, then took her by the arm to direct her toward the exit. "Take your purse. You're coming with me."

In her reverie, Stacey must have missed some key information but, trusting the girls, she picked up her handbag, followed Annie to the exit and headed down the street. A few minutes later, Françoise caught up with them, and a few minutes after that, Corinne arrived, running, pushing them all.

"Go!" she cried out. "Get moving!"

And all four took off, running after Corinne as she took a left, then a right down a narrow street, then another left, and came to a halt. The girls all laughed, as Corinne peered back around the street corner.

"We're good," she said.

The girls laughed some more, this time from relief. Her heart pounding, Stacey was only starting to catch her breath when realization hit.

"You left without paying!" It came out harsher than she meant, accusatory.

The girls looked at one another and burst out laughing. "No, *you* left without paying."

"But that's stealing."

"And 8 Euros for a coffee isn't stealing?" more laughter.

Their laughter was infectious. Stacey smiled. They jostled one another, then jostled her and gave her a little push in the right direction.

"*C'est pas grave,*" said Annie.

And Françoise, "That's just the first of the evening's adventures!" The girls laughed again, hooted even, and Corinne winked at her. "Let's get a move on. We've got a full agenda."

After walking ten minutes and making a few more right-left moves, the group arrived in the rue Saint Denis, a pedestrian street filled with shops; or maybe "boutiques" is a better word since most were small and funky, except that "boutique" tends to mean high-end and the merchandise here most certainly was not. Since the weather was good, most of the shops had moved racks out onto the sidewalk to better tempt the passersby. In front of one store were two rows of headless mannequins, lined up like the Queen's Guards in front of Buckingham Palace, if the guards were allowed to wear loud stripes, Hawaiian print or backless halter dresses.

The girls moved from shop to shop, from item to item, exclaiming over this, enthralled by that. Françoise held a blouse in front of her, said something that Stacey didn't catch, and Annie and Corrine burst out laughing. Stacey followed along, enjoying their infectious good humor despite being jostled now and then in the crowded street. After a little while, she even started participating herself, finding a hideous yellow caftan at the used clothes store.

She held it up and called out to Corinne, "Hey, this would look good on you." Corinne looked horrified. The other two tittered. Stacey found a pair of creole earrings, hoops the size of her hand. Holding them up to her ear, she asked, "I dunno, is my neck long enough?"

The fun continued, each boutique a new opportunity for jokes until they reached a store with what Stacey took to be a series of small paintings.

Why on earth would you paint such beautiful images on cardboard, she wondered. She understood her mistake when Annie pointed to one of the drawings and then to her wrist, which bore the same image. As a mother, Stacey was horrified; the idea of someone drawing on flesh made her skin crawl. As an art lover, however, she had to admit that some of the drawings were, indeed, beautiful. On cardboard.

The three girls pointed excitedly at something in a flat glass display case. Looking over their shoulders, Stacey saw some of the same piercings her daughter wore: some simple hoops, studs, studs with skulls, two balls separated by a long shaft for the belly button. She felt reasonably hip since she recognized most of the pieces, yet felt the generation gap as well since she just didn't understand the attraction. These three girls, her daughter too, were all very pretty. Why would they choose to mutilate themselves with these things? Stacey was from a generation raised with the adage "You need it like a hole in the head." This younger generation was choosing to have *multiple* holes in the head!

The girls interrupted Stacey's musings by heading down the street toward a shop with a display of cardboard legs, showing off the different tights and nylons sold inside, some legs up, some legs down, a gaudy multicolored chorus line. The girls lined up in front of the cardboard legs and performed their own French cancan, falling over with laughter at their own daring before the shop girl shooed them off.

As they rambled on, the shops grew sparser and they came upon the *Passage du Cerf*, the Deer's Passage. Paris has quite a few covered passages left. These passages dating from the 18th century were the precursors to today's shopping malls. The *Passage du Cerf* was narrow, the width of a small compact car, not two, although now it was only open to pedestrians so it didn't matter. The old-fashioned wooden store fronts rose up two floors before ending in a graceful glass ceiling which protected both the shoppers and the grey, black and white checkerboard tiles from the rain. Stepping into the *Passage du Cerf* was like taking a step back in time, to a moment when life was more graceful. While the Rue Saint Denis was funky, the shops here were artsy: a fabric store, artisan soaps, vintage eye glasses, and several jewelers who sold only their own creations. It was, to quote the Lindt commercial, a few grams of refinement in a world of brutes.

As if to complete this moment of beauty, a young man started singing a Gregorian chant as he walked slowly down the passage, stopping here and there to test the acoustic. *How lovely!* Stacey thought. Corinne snored in mockery.

Stacey was in her element here; the girls, however, were bored, so they hurried on, out the passage and down the street. A block or so further on, Annie stopped in front of a bar which had a series of free postcards on an outdoor rack, a common way for Parisian establishments to advertise themselves. The cards, however, weren't common at all. "Look at this!" Annie exclaimed as she held one up. The postcard showed a photo of a man, well-built, muscular, completely nude, holding a glass and a bottle of champagne while strategically positioned behind a pink flamingo. The girls snickered and laughed. Stacey, feeling like the responsible adult in the group, averted her gaze. As she looked around, her eyes lit on a building across the street and realization dawned on her.

"That's why the sexy postcards," she said.

"Why?" replied Françoise, examining another one of the cards more closely.

Stacey nodded toward the mansion across the street. Françoise barely looked at it, preferring the young man on the card, until Stacey said, "That was one of the biggest brothels in Paris in the 18th century."

"What?!" That got their attention. All three girls were looking at her now, waiting expectantly for more, so Stacey explained: how, at the time, the mansion was located just outside of Paris city limits, the frontier between legal and illegal for prostitution at the time; how noblemen would come there for "entertainment;" how the woman who would become King Louis XV's favorite mistress practiced her trade there before using her influence on the king to become the *Comtesse du Barry*.

The girls listened to the history lesson, enthralled, then Annie asked, "Cool. How do you know all this?"

How indeed? Stacey thought back to a time, years before, when Jean had taken her on a tour of Paris, visiting a series of places which Jean clearly found titillating and Stacey, sordid. Had he tried to reach out to her that day? Did her negative reaction drive him to find someone else who was more—how to say—interested in the subject?

She couldn't possibly share this with the girls. Stacey tore herself away from these thoughts and replied, somewhat self-consciously, "I don't know. I just don't know how I know this."

But Annie, like life, had moved on already. "Time waits for no one," as the saying went, nor did three young women. Françoise was already chatting about "a really cool place" she had seen, "not far at all." She led the way, the other girls hovering around her like electrons to a nucleus. As the group walked, Françoise continued to describe the wonderful scenes they were about to see, building up their excitement more and more.

Suddenly, she stopped, pointed to a nondescript building across the street and said, "There it is."

5

Graffiti

THE OTHERS LOOKED at a perfect example of 1970's build-it-fast utilitarian architecture. If there were an architect involved, that is. You couldn't say it was ugly, because "ugly" had more character than the building they were looking at. The girls looked confused, while Stacey felt disappointed after all the wonders Françoise had described, and Françoise, paying no attention to the others, crossed the street and walked in the front door.

The others followed. As soon as they crossed the

threshold, a miracle happened; they were transported into another world, full of color, light and design. Graffiti, paintings, everywhere, literally, everywhere: the walls, floors, ceilings, doors, doorknobs, even the vents of the heating system were covered in paint, sometimes by multiple layers of paint, or images printed on paper glued over the painted designs. It was truly wonderful, just as Françoise had said.

The building itself had a simple design: a central foyer with one hallway extending to the left and another to the right, a line of doors on both sides of the hallways, a stairway at the outer end of each hallway, the same pattern repeated floor after floor. Every surface on every floor was covered in "graffiti." Graffiti? Paintings? "Street art" could work, except that these were inside, not out on the street. It was everywhere and so outside of anything Stacey had ever experienced that she didn't know the proper words to describe it.

That, too, was new for Stacey, not to have the words to describe something. It was not a museum, as Corinne kept telling her, trying to urge her to go faster. It was... It was an art gallery on steroids. It was the Louvre with its entire collection packed into one room. It was an archeological site you could excavate and understand only after weeks, months, years. It was an onion you needed to peel away layer by layer.

It was... Stacey gave up.

She was caught up in the images, by their power, sometimes simply by their sheer number. Density, maybe, was a better word, since every square inch was covered and sometimes covered several times since a painting could be partially covered with paper prints, which were in turn partially painted. She had never seen so much art in one place before.

She gave up trying to describe it, to understand it, or even to keep track of where they were in the building and let herself be swept away by the tsunami of emotions the art created in her.

The entry way had one wall covered in a riff on Angry Birds, brightly colored in pink, blue, yellow and green, sitting in a white bowl filled with Chinese noodles on a black background. Next to it were paintings of what looked like two pieces of African primitive art, female, facing one another. The statues were rendered with such a realistic 3-D effect that Stacey felt she could turn them around to see the other profile. Facing this, was a surrealistic sea scape in gloomy hues, a painted mash-up of Salvador Dali and Jules Verne. Stacey was contemplating these works when Françoise took her by the arm and gently pushed her toward the hallway on the left.

"You gotta keep up," she scolded. "There's a lot more to see and this" -- she gestured to the entrance walls-- "isn't the best stuff."

Right away, Stacey was a little annoyed to be rushed like this. Later, she had to admit Françoise was right. There was so very much to see and this wasn't the best work.

Stacey moved on, following Françoise. At first, she tried to keep track of where they were, then little by little gave up as she became entranced by the designs, no, the universes, which talented young painters had created.

She entered two evocations of the death camps in Nazi Germany, one rendered realistically with rows of skulls atop wood and stone. The other, an oddly cheerful yellow, green, blue and grey background festooned with black blobs in which you could see just enough bones to know if it was the head, thorax or pelvis and legs. Despite the bright colors, the result was strangely eerie, more disturbing than the realistic version.

A few feet further on, Stacey entered into a psychedelic universe. Multiple shades of coral, pink, yellow, and turquoise blobby things, highlighted with various shades of purple, extended from the walls onto the floor and the ceiling, so that Stacey felt as if she were in the middle of a lava lamp, pulsing with its happiness and suspended mid-air (mid-art?).

A few more steps jolted her into a radically different world. The hallway was painted only in red, white and black, bold, stylized graphics evoking ships and the sea, both modern and masculine. Then, Stacey was carried to Africa, with floor to ceiling portraits of African women in native dress, their grace, beauty and magnetism creating a traffic jam among the visitors. Seeing them, Stacey stood a little taller, a little straighter, unconsciously adopting their majestic pose. A beam supporting the ceiling proclaimed "Diversity is hope." The visitors, just below, unwittingly illustrated the point.

From there, a lush garden, highly unrealistic yet inviting. It made Stacey think of Disney's version of *Alice in Wonderland* and what might have happened if the illustrators had been free to let it rip. She wanted to meet the caterpillar and smoke his hookah with him. She was already in a delirium... an art-induced delirium.

A series of Japanese line drawings, precise yet cold, led the way to cityscapes halfway covered by paint drippings. As she strolled on, these were replaced by an alarm clock evocation of Stephane Hessel's great work, which gave way to a stairway, so covered in geometric patterns she could no longer determine where the stairs were or how high to raise her feet.

The images assaulted Stacey and overwhelmed her, yet she grabbed at them and the feelings they elicited. Like waves pounding the beach, the images crashed on her again and again. She had never experienced anything so intense in her entire life and was enjoying feeling so overwhelmed by art.

She came to a dead end, a blank wall, the first blank wall in what felt like ages. The girls were waiting for her, hands on hips, impatient.

They had seen it, done it and were ready to move on.

There is an impatience in youth, thought Stacey. Perhaps the good side of getting older (not that she was old by any means, but, let's face it, she wasn't twenty anymore), the good side of getting older is that you take the time to savor, to really appreciate things. Like good art, even if it takes the form of graffiti on the walls of an abandoned building in the center of Paris.

6

Picnic

"WHERE TO NEXT?" asked Stacey, as they emerged from the building and Stacey emerged from the artistic haze.

It was starting to get late, nearing nine o'clock; and the stores were now closed. All but one, the corner *épicerie*, also known as the *"Arabe du coin,"* since such stores were often held by people who came from or whose parents came from North Africa, in the timeless, universal tradition of immigrants holding down the jobs that no one else wanted. The Arab in the Corner Store was hard working, open during the day and most of the night, supplying the sugar you just ran out of, the cheese you forgot to buy, or the bottle of wine you would bring to the friends who invited you over at the last minute.

The store itself was surprising. All the products you found in a supermarket were jam-packed into a space no larger than your living room, like a life-size 3D puzzle or Ali Baba's cavern chock full of canned peas and bags of pasta instead of diamonds and rubies. Reaching up to the ceiling, the shelves were so tightly packed with so many varieties of food stuffs that the word "optimization" was inadequate. "Beyond optimization"?

The girls and Stacey entered the *épicerie* with the same exuberance they had for the clothes shops. Françoise headed toward the wine section.

Picking up two bottles, almost at random, she turned to the others and asked, "Red, or rosé?" showing each bottle in turn. When Annie picked up a bag of chips, Stacey cringed.

"No, no, no," she said, taking the chips out of Annie's hands and placing them back on the rack. "You girls know fashion and beauty. I know food." She made a quick tour of the shop, picked out some nice olives, a pack of cherry tomatoes, a well-aged brie, some pâté and a baguette, putting each item in Annie's hands before heading over to

Françoise and choosing two bottles of a different wine. On second thought... she handed the wine to Françoise then picked up two more bottles and headed to the cash register.

"Do you have a cork screw?" she asked.

The shopkeeper pulled out a small metal cork screw from under the counter. "Three Euros."

Stacey nodded her approval. "A knife and napkins?"

The shopkeeper pulled out a plastic knife and a small stack of paper napkins, adding them to the knife with a smile. "On the house."

As he rang up her purchases, Stacey couldn't help but think of a novel she had read, *Monsieur Ibrahim et les fleurs du Coran* in which the Arab on the Corner was actually Jewish and his business plan could be summarized as "buy for one, sell for two." Given the prices indicated on the cash register in front of her, this shopkeeper must have multiplied by three or four. But what the hell? She felt in her pocket, took out the two fifty euro bills she had placed there earlier when she had argued with Madame Pipi, and handed them over.

As the young women bagged their groceries, Stacey put the change into her pocket and asked, "Where are we going to have our picnic?"

Instead of answering, Corinne took one bottle out of the sack, opened it up, took a sip, and passed the bottle to

Stacey, who did the same, handing the bottle to Annie. Drinking, walking, sharing stories of other evenings out, the group moved from the pedestrian street to smaller streets, around the corner, into the entrance of a building, through the courtyard and out the building on the other side, onto a street so narrow it must have been built in the middle ages. Stacey spread open her arms and almost reached both sides with her hands. She looked up at the façades which bowed outward, making the distance across the street even narrower as they rose skyward. She smiled to herself. Even after all these years in France, she still wasn't used to how old things were here.

As if to confirm her thoughts, the group turned onto the *Rue Montorgueil* and passed in front of a bakery, the *Pâtisserie Stohrer, "Maison fondée en 1730,"* the sign proudly proclaimed.

1730! thought Stacey. They were making croissants 43 years before the Boston Tea Party, and 46 years before the Declaration of Independence!

By this time, Corinne had opened the second bottle. Either the wine, or the ambiance of the pedestrian street, was having an effect on Stacey. She felt as if she was playing a Parisian treasure hunt. After the historic bakery, she found a restaurant sporting a 3-foot tall golden snail over its entrance. And there, above the awning of a sidewalk café, she saw a cross between a painting and a comic strip. Just as the stained glass windows in cathedrals were intended to teach the word of God to the illiterate churchgoers, the painting on the café's façade showed passersby how good the food was inside.

A few steps further, the group rounded the corner of the Église Saint Eustache and came upon a stone esplanade showcasing what looked like two round boulders, one larger than the other. On closer inspection, they saw that the larger boulder was a head; the smaller one, a hand, facing it. The proportions were enormous. The nostril alone was bigger than Stacey's entire head. She began singing a little ditty from childhood, "Put your finger up your nose, up your nose."

The girls stopped and listened. When she got to the punchline, "and it will stretch like pantyhose," they exploded with laughter.

"Looks like it already did," commented Françoise, to renewed hilarity. Corinne took a photo of Annie splayed on the palm of the hand, then another of Stacey angling her head as if to enter the nostril, as she wiped tears of laughter from her eyes. It had been a long, long time since Stacey had laughed this hard and felt this free.

The esplanade led to a large grassy field bordered by long benches in the same stone as the esplanade's pavers

"This is ideal," declared Corinne, as she placed her grocery bag on the grass and plunked down next to it. Stacey and the other two girls followed suit, spreading their picnic out on the grass, Stacey cutting off chunks of cheese, Annie tearing pieces of *baguette*, Françoise helping herself to an olive before passing the jar to Corinne, who was busy opening the third bottle of wine.

Stacey asked Françoise about the building they had just seen with all that graffiti. "Are you a fan of street art?" she asked.

"Not just," Françoise answered. "I like art in general."

"Yeah," chimed in Corinne, "we're always pulling her out of museums to go have fun."

"Oh really?" murmured Stacey.

"Yes, I've studied art quite a bit."

"And yet," Stacey paused, not sure how to continue without hurting Françoise's feelings.

"And yet I work at Sephora?" Françoise did it for her, smiling. "My parents think the same thing. I'm a salesperson at Sephora but they hired me for my make-up artist skills."

"You're really good at it," Stacey added. "I've tested."

"Well, I'm good at it because I'm actually pretty good at painting. And drawing."

Annie chimed in, "Oooh, remember those drawings

she did after we went to the horse races? They were so beautiful!"

Annie and Corinne described the different paintings Françoise had created, often during outings that the three young women did together. They were proud of their friend, of her talent, and clearly expected she would one day live from her art.

"How about you, Annie?" Stacey asked. "Do you have artistic dreams, too?"

"Oh no!" exclaimed Annie. "I've already realized my dream: to become a hair stylist. Ever since I was a little girl, that's all I ever wanted to be. And I am!"

"Don't you want something more?" asked Stacey, thinking of Jean and most of her friends, who had achieved a high level of success yet were continually striving (grasping?) for more. More, more, always more.

Annie laughed. "I know, everybody asks me that. But the fact is that I am happy right now. I enjoy my work, I love my clients, and I take classes regularly to stay abreast of the latest techniques. You have to keep up with the times, you know." Stacey had to laugh at that last comment, someone so young wanting to keep up with the times.

"What about you, Corinne?" Stacey asked.

Corinne, usually so confident and sure of herself, went

silent. Annie had "arrived," Françoise had a plan, and Corinne, the star of the little group, said nothing.

Françoise came to her rescue. "There's nothing wrong with selling clothes."

"Of course not," Stacey replied, realizing she had inadvertently touched a sore subject. "Especially when you're so good at it. You have a knack for picking out just the right clothes to flatter one's figure, the right form and the right color. I would never have chosen that mustard blouse—and now it's my favorite."

Corinne looked pleased so Stacey continued, "I hate clothes shopping; nothing's ever in my size or looks right on me. And the saleswomen! Some of them must think I'm stupid or they would never tell me I look good in that outfit." The girls chortled. "I looked like a sausage!"

Corinne cracked up. "I see that a lot; women who can't bear to accept a size larger than what they've always worn. You'd think their dress size was tattooed on their foreheads! Or their identity defined by that single number."

"And yet," Stacey continued, "you were honest with me, you advised me well, I had a good time and, more importantly, every time I wear the clothes you chose, people compliment me and I feel like a million bucks." Corinne beamed with pride. "You are a really good salesman. Maybe you could consider selling higher priced items where you would earn more money."

"Yeah," Annie chimed in. "Like cars."

"Or houses," Françoise added. "Or yachts."

"Ooh! We could have so much fun if you sold yachts!" Annie exclaimed. "I'd come to help with the test drive!"

"Or," Stacey interjected, "since you are also very good with clothes, maybe try for a job at one of the *haute couture* shops in Paris. If that's too snobby for you, what about personal shopper at the Galerie Lafayette or Le Printemps?"

Corinne's eyes lit up. "I would enjoy that! I could help people not just on one day but over a period of time—that is how you construct a good wardrobe, you know, over time."

Stacey could see the wheels turning in Corinne's head, glad to see the girl's excitement. *You needed to be excited about life*, Stacey thought, *especially when you're young and have so much ahead of you*. Although now that she thought about it, she needed some excitement, too. Get out of her humdrum everyday life. Of course, this past month, all her scheming and revenge had done just that. It would probably be better, though, if her excitement came from a positive, constructive project—and something she was good at— something more like Françoise's passion for art.

Stacey's thoughts wandered to Jean. Maybe Jean had extra-marital affairs because he needed some excitement, too, and didn't have enough imagination—or enough understanding of who Stacey really was—to create it with her.

The group, already jolly, became merrier as they worked their way through the meal and the remaining wine. The conversation had moved on, leaving the subject of their futures to stories of other evenings out and tales of daring and adventure during those evenings out. The girls had so much to say! Stacey remained quiet, listening to the others and their tall tales.

"What about you, Stacey?" asked Françoise.

"There's not a lot to tell," she replied. "I've lived longer than you three, but I'm beginning to wonder if I've lived as much."

"There's still time to fix that," said Corinne, a twinkle in her eye. She got to her feet. "Let's go."

The girls disposed of their trash, then followed Corinne who walked past a large domed building toward what looked like a kids' playground.

7

Kids' park

MORE THAN A playground," the sign promised. "A terrain of adventures." Stacey liked the sound of that.

Corinne easily hopped the fence, then turned around and motioned for Stacey to follow. As Stacey hesitated, Annie took her handbag from her and passed it to Corinne over the chained link.

"The park's closed," Stacey protested.

"I just reopened it," replied Corinne.

"The sign says it's for kids eight to twelve years old."

"Aren't you really a child at heart?" Corinne smiled. Stacey laughed. It was hard to beat that logic.

Annie put her hands together to give Stacey a step up. It was as easy as that: Stacey went up and over the fence, landing squarely in Adventure Land.

A long, ivy-covered tunnel, cut the rectangular park lengthwise; on the left were low mosaic-covered rock-climbing walls and grass for playing soccer. On the right was a series of high-tech playground equipment, tightly packed to maximize space, fitting together like pieces of a puzzle. A rainbow bridge, both rainbow colored and rainbow shaped, created an area for hide and seek and more rock-climbing underneath. Two spherical jungle gyms, one stacked on top of the other, led to a double-helix metal slide which spiraled around the balls to end in the grass. There were swings, rope bridges, tetherballs on their poles. It was all here and more. Corinne tapped Stacey on the shoulder then pointed to the top of the slide.

"I dare you! I double-dare you!" she exclaimed. In her inebriated state, Stacey didn't need more to egg her on. She ducked into the bottom sphere and started climbing, actually elbowing Corinne in her hurry, yelling "Ta da!" when she reached the top, to Corinne's cries of "You cheater!" Both women burst out laughing, before gliding down the slides, landing on their feet, ready for another go-round.

They played and played, not a care in the world, until Stacey, a little tired, rested on the swings, a little mesmerized by the rhythmical rocking, a little dazed but happy. She was having a lot of fun with the threesome. Soon, the girls were played out too, and ready to move on.

And so they did.

Part of the fun in hopping the fence to go into the playground came from breaking the rules. Hopping out didn't hold the same appeal.

8

Laundromat

CORRINE MUST HAVE sensed Stacey's mood because she bumped her shoulder against Stacey's, smiled and said, "Don't worry. The fun's not over yet."

They ducked down a side street which was narrower and darker, the only light coming from a storefront halfway down the street. When they reached the store, neon lights glaring through the floor-to-ceiling windows made it look like an aquarium. Stacey saw that it was a laundromat. The group stopped.

"We're here," Corinne announced, with a smile.

"Oooh, the dryer!" Annie and Françoise sang out together, as they pushed Stacey through the front door.

A laundromat? The scene of their next adventure? What—they're going to make sure that the machines wash whiter than white?

As could be expected at this hour, they were alone. The girls made a beeline to the dryers, choosing the oversize one made for drying sleeping bags, bed spreads, and those big, bulky duvets.

"In you go," Annie said to Stacey as she motioned to the gaping maw of the dryer.

"What?" Stacey exclaimed. "Are you crazy?"

The three young women just laughed. Then, seeing that Stacey wouldn't budge, Corinne exclaimed, "It's really fun. I know it seems bizarre, but it's really fun. You're gonna have to trust us."

Stacey did trust Corinne but was still unsure. "It's not going to hurt me?"

"Of course not!" Corinne replied. "Now, put your butt in first." Stacey complied.

"Watch your head," Françoise said as she put her hand on Stacey's head, like a cop putting a criminal into the back seat of a patrol car. "Now your feet." She bent down, grasped both of Stacey's feet and shoved them in. Stacey found herself curled into a ball, her back shaped like a C along the drum of the dryer, her arms and legs fit in as best they could. Luckily, it was industrial-sized, but even so there wasn't a lot of spare room.

"Are you ready?"

She couldn't imagine for what, but answered "yes" all the same.

"*Et c'est parti!*" Off we go! exclaimed Corinne as she pushed on one of the cross pieces on the inside wall. The drum started to turn. Annie and Françoise pushed on the cross pieces as well, as the drum picked up speed and Stacey found herself spinning, head over heels, slowly at first then faster and faster, laughing from exhilaration. She thought of a hamster in its exercise wheel which sometimes got a little too much momentum and ended up doing a flip. This was so fun! Almost like a ride in an amusement park. Maybe when the hamster did his flip it wasn't an accident. Maybe he did it on purpose just for fun?

Stacey spun and laughed and then, little by little, the girls slowed her down and brought the dryer to a halt. As soon as the dryer stopped spinning, her head started. Slowly, carefully, she moved one foot out of the dryer, then the whole leg, next foot, next leg, then hands and head. Before her feet could touch the ground, she clutched at both sides of the dryer, head reeling.

The girls laughed. "It'll stop in a few minutes," Corinne reassured her. "Do you want to sit there on the edge for a while?"

"*Non!*" cried Annie. "She can sit over there," pointing to a bench on the side of the laundromat. "It's my turn."

Stacey had to laugh. These kids! Carefully, she moved out of the way and sat on top of a nearby washer from where she could watch the trio take turns going for a dryer ride. Just as Corinne had predicted, Stacey's dizziness dissipated little by little and, by the time the girls were ready to go, she was, too.

"Where to now?" she asked, ready for the next adventure.

9

The fountain

THE FOUNTAIN," Corinne replied.

"The fountain?"

"The fountain!" Annie and Françoise exclaimed.

Clearly, they had done this before. "You're going to love it!" added Françoise.

The group hurried out of the laundromat and down the street. After walking a few minutes, they arrived at a town square, which was, actually, a big square instead of the usual circle, a rare enough occurrence in Paris for Stacey to notice. Around the edges of the square, on all four sides, were three steps, leading upward. In the center, a round basin framing the fountain itself: a square structure, all four sides the same, composed of five half-moon stairs leading gracefully upward to an elongated arch, topped by a horizontal pediment, then a dome, and finally a spire. There was an upward movement in the fountain, reaching skyward, despite its heavy stone structure.

Corinne, Annie, and Françoise were already wading into the basin, playing with the water as it cascaded down the crescent stairs, splashing one another. For once, Stacey didn't hesitate. Not waiting to be invited, she jumped over the small wall of the basin and landed with a splash. And a giggle. She had fallen back into childhood on the swing set in the park, before arriving here, to this fountain. The real fountain of youth, however, was spending time with these vibrant young women and allowing herself to act and react completely in the moment, without worrying about tomorrow, or the dirty laundry in the hamper, or the kids waiting for their dinner. Wait a minute! It was late now. Did the kids get any dinner? Of course they did! They were with their friends.

Annie interrupted Stacey's train of thought by filling a paper cup full of water and throwing it at her. The water exploded over her blouse.

Corinne cried out, "Stacey just won the wet t-shirt

contest!" Stacey laughed and splashed water back at Annie before ducking behind the corner of the fountain to sneak around and attack from behind.

Before long, all four were drenched.

Françoise, no longer caring, sat down on one of the half-moon stairs and languorously rested her elbows on the higher step behind her, totally unconcerned by the water running down the stairs and over her back and legs.

Stacey, tired but exhilarated, sat next to Annie and Corinne on the edge of the basin, feet dangling in the water, talking a little but mainly basking in the camaraderie of the moment.

Stacey remembered a time, years ago, when Laura was a little girl. They were waiting in line to enter the Louvre, the line snaking far from the metal and glass pyramid which housed the entrance. There were a lot of visitors that day. The kids were already bored, and they hadn't even entered the place. Stacey was bored, too, and her mind must have wandered because, suddenly, she heard people laughing and saw them pointing at—Laura! Laura had climbed into one of the triangular reflecting pools and was making her way to the circle of water jets in the middle, picking up coins the tourists had thrown in as she moved forward.

"Laura!" Stacey called out. In panic? In embarrassment? She felt like such a bad mother, like all those people in the line must think she was a bad mother. "Laura! Come back here right now."

Laura turned to her mother, pure joy on her little five-year-old face. "Look, Mommy, I found a penny." She held up a single coin for her mother to see. "A real American penny. I'm going to be lucky all day."

Stacey scolded Laura who reluctantly left the fountain, tearfully abandoning her handful of coins but stubbornly holding on to her lucky penny.

All these years later, Stacey relived the scene, seeing the little girl's transformation from joy to tears, and wondered if she had done the right thing. Sure, it had been the responsible thing to do , but maybe it would have been better to let Laura have her little adventure just as she, Stacey, was having an adventure tonight. Maybe discovery and experimentation are really all that matter? Stacey laughed at herself. "Discovery." "Experimentation." That was what responsible adults said when what they really meant was "play."

Kids didn't need to make it all serious and grandiloquent. They just played, which was what Stacey and the girls were doing right now.

"Isn't Nico going to wonder where you are?" Annie asked Corinne.

"Yeah, probably," she replied. She glanced at her

watch and started to get to her feet. "We should probably get going. They'll be finished soon."

Stacey didn't really pay attention to this conversation, merely following suit as Annie and Françoise also got up and started walking down the street.

10

Shopping carts

THEY WALKED LONG enough for Stacey to dry off almost completely but not so long as to wear off the warm glow—of the wine? Of the playtime? She didn't know. She simply felt good. She remembered Mrs. Herring, her high school English teacher, saying all good literature was about human suffering; when you were happy, you didn't analyze it, you just enjoyed it. There was nothing to say.

It had taken Stacey thirty years and this very unusual evening to be able to say, "Mrs. Herring was right."

She felt happy. She just wanted to enjoy it.

Maybe there is nothing more to say but there is definitely more to do, thought Stacey as she spotted a derelict shopping cart on the side of the street. She took hold of the handle and pushed it frontward and backward, turned it left and right to test its dynamics. It was all right. The girls watched her, bemused.

"Who wants to get in first?" asked Stacey.

Since no one answered, she rolled the cart up to Corinne.

"Get in."

Corinne didn't budge. "Remember when you said to trust you with the dryer? And I did? Well, I'm asking you to trust me now."

Corinne, bemused, didn't say anything as she climbed into the cart, resting her back against the back wall, feet facing forward. Stacey plunked her purse into the cart, next to Corinne.

"You might want to hold on," she said, before starting to run and push the cart with all her might. Corinne hooted. Annie and Françoise hurried to keep up. Once she had gained enough momentum, Stacey gave the handle a sharp push to the left and let go. The cart spun around 360°. Stacey reached out to stop it and run some more.

"You're crazy!" shouted Annie.

A few minutes later, after a few more spins, some slaloming, and skidding, Stacey was out of breath. She brought the shopping cart to a halt and helped Corinne get out. Corinne was tripping over herself, she was laughing so hard.

"Oh my God!" she cried. "That was so much fun! Where did you learn that?"

"Learn?" Stacey feigned incomprehension. "I was born with this talent."

The girls laughed some more. As Stacey's breathing came back to normal, Françoise asked "Can I have a turn?" Stacey gave a ride to both Françoise and Annie, catching her breath each time between riders. After a while, though, Corinne looked at her watch and said, "We gotta get moving. We're going to be late."

Stacey was proud of herself. She, too, had contributed something to the evening's adventures.

Quietly content, she followed the girls who were busy chattering, still laughing and joking as they had done all evening but with a slightly different tone, an edge that Stacey didn't quite understand. Then she heard Annie mention several names, all masculine. *Ah, that's it!* thought Stacey. *We're going to see the boyfriends.*

11

Busking

THE LITTLE GROUP turned onto a pedestrian street filled with restaurants, bars and sidewalk cafés. Everyone was out enjoying the beautiful summer weather.

It was one of the things Stacey liked about Paris—all of France for that matter. As soon as the *beaux jours* arrived, night life was transferred to the out of doors, often as late as midnight or 2 am. Of course, she didn't want a café for a neighbor, but it was a nice custom.

Midway down the street was a small band—singer,

guitarist and drummer—performing in between a restaurant where patrons were finishing their late dinner and a bar, with those out for a drink. At the end of the song, the girls raced up to their boyfriends, each kissing her own *mec* on the lips before giving the usual greeting of the *bise*, a peck on both cheeks, to the others.

"Stacey, this is Nico, Seb and Alex," Corinne said, motioning to each young man in turn. "Guys, this is Stacey. She's a friend of ours from the mall." One by one, the young men greeted Stacey with a *bise*, then told the girls they wanted to perform a few more songs before breaking up for the evening.

"Can we sing back-up like we did last week?" asked Françoise.

"Of course," replied Nico.

And so Stacey found herself in a chorus line with the three young women, sharing a microphone, singing back-up to a series of rock 'n roll classics: Beatles, David Bowie, Queen, the Blues Brothers (ok, not the Blues Brothers but songs from the sound track). Stacey had never sung in public before, only in the shower or alone in the car, but, between all that wine and the camaraderie with these girls, she felt confident. She was having fun. She was in the zone.

So much so that, when the boys played "Respect," she

felt she was channeling her inner Aretha. Dancing around the mike, belting out "R-E-S-P-E-C-T, find out what that means to me." She was a diva. She was the Queen.

Suddenly, she realized, she was also alone.

She was the only one singing.

The boys continued to play the instrumentals, but the girls had taken two steps backward, leaving her alone at the mike, dancing a little choreography behind her.

She panicked.

Oh my God! she thought, I'm the only one singing! At my age! I'm ridiculous!

Glancing at the audience, looking over at the band members, she saw them all smiling, clearly enjoying her surprise performance. Even so, she panicked and her mind went blank.

Seb, the lead singer, noticed she missed the next lyrics. He walked over to her, put an arm encouragingly around her shoulder and sang into the mike "Ooo, your kisses, sweeter than honey. And guess what? So is my money." It was just the encouragement Stacey needed. She joined him, and they finished the song as a duo, to roaring applause. The girls rushed back to cheer her. The drummer beat his two drumsticks together. Seb gave her a big hug, before moving back to his own microphone.

"With that great performance by Stacey, ladies and

gentlemen, we end our show for tonight. If you enjoyed it, please remember to leave a little something in the hat," he said, as he pointed to a hat containing a few bills and coins at his feet.

The girls were talking excitedly, all at once.

"Oh my God! I didn't know you could sing like that," exclaimed Françoise.

"*Une triomphe!*" cried Annie.

"Sock it to me," laughed Corinne, giving Stacey a small punch on the shoulder.

12

Paris at her feet

THE BOYS PACKED up their gear and stored it in a back room of the bar. Evidently they had an agreement with the bar's owner, free storage for free entertainment. Evidently, too, their music brought in extra business. Stacey noticed several of the bar's patrons leaving as soon as the music had finished. Once all their equipment was safely stored, the young men were ready to move.

"What do you want to do?" Seb asked Stacey.

"She's on a quest," Corinne interrupted.

"A quest?"

"Yes. Her husband is cheating on her. Her kids are shits." Seeing Stacey make a face, Corinne corrected herself, "OK, maybe they're not shits, but they're teenagers which is more or less the same thing."

Françoise broke in. "Stacey has been too good for too long."

Annie had to add her two *centimes*, too. "She's been a nice wife and mother for years and years and years. Even her revenge is too nice!"

"We promised her fun," Françoise said.

"And adventure," Annie added.

"That's her quest," Corinne said.

Hearing this, her life's story summarized so succinctly and so publicly, Stacey felt embarrassed. Seb made no comment, no sniggering.

After a few minutes of reflection, he simply said, "I know where you need to go."

With that, the group took off, the three girls, the three boys, and one middle-aged woman, out for adventure.

Seb, like Corinne earlier in the evening, walked like a gangster drives when he wants to shake a tail: a left here, a right there, speed up, slow down. Suddenly, he stopped short, declaring, "We're here."

We're where? thought Stacey. They were on a perfectly

normal sidewalk, on a perfectly normal street, not many people out at this time of night since this was an office district. As far as Stacey could see, there was no more reason to stop here than, say, at that other corner other there. The only difference she could see was the scaffolding in front of an office building.

It was exactly that scaffolding which interested Seb. He ducked under the safety netting, grabbed ahold of the metal flooring above his head and hoisted himself up to the next level. The girls and Nico followed suit, using the little knobby outcroppings on the vertical bars as footholds and handholds.

They're crazy, Stacey thought. *I can't do this,* as she watched the others scamper up like mountain goats. She remembered gym class, back in the day, with the annual rope-climbing test. Year after year, she had been forced to face the fact that she had no upper body strength. The one year she actually succeeded in climbing up the damn rope, she learned that what she lacked in upper body strength she made up for in vertigo.

"No, I can't do this."

She must have said it out loud because Alex, bringing up the rear, answered her.

"It's not as hard as it looks. Here, let me take your handbag," he said as he deftly took her purse and slung it across his shoulder.

He patiently explained how to use the "knobby things," the place where workers could attach horizontal beams to the vertical bars, to place her foot so it wouldn't slip. She could push on her legs and use the force of her legs, not her arms, to climb steadily higher, her hands merely guiding the way.

Alex gently coached her up first one flight of scaffolding, then another, and again and again, until they reached the rooftop where they found the others, sitting or lying on an oh so Parisian grey metal roof. Alex took Stacey's hand to guide her to the ridge, where the two eaves came together, to the highest point where she could see Paris, 360°.

Alex took a flask out of his pocket. The others came closer to share the flask and to point out the Parisian landmarks to Stacey.

It was spectacular.

Paris really was the City of Lights, one of the great beauties in this world. You could enjoy the view from level three of the Eiffel Tower or from the dome of *Sacré Coeur*, but you could appreciate Paris best only after risking your life by climbing six stories up the outside of a building. Stacey had been afraid, had conquered her fear with the help of Alex, and now all of Paris lay at her feet. Literally.

13

The hotel

THE PROVERB "all things that go up must come down" was as true of rooftop tourists as it was of cannonballs. After half an hour of admiring the view, after Alex's flask ran out, the group climbed back down to the ground. Was it that she now had experience? Was it the grain alcohol from the flask? Stacey found the way down much easier.

She thought about David who had wanted to go rock climbing with his mom and sister last year. Stacey had quickly squashed that idea. Now, she wondered if he'd still be interested. After all, if she could climb up the outside of a building, she could surely climb up a specially designed wall while wearing a security harness.

Success breeding success? Or was adventure, like revenge, addictive?

Back at street level, Françoise suggested to the others that they all go to a nightclub to dance. Everyone approved the idea, everyone except Stacey who was beginning to feel her age.

"Not for me," she said, with a little glance at her watch. It was well after one. "I'm feeling tired, so I'll leave you here."

"We can do something else," offered Françoise, not wanting to leave Stacey out, although Corinne and Annie looked disappointed.

"I've had such a good time with you, but I really need to get some sleep. You kids go on and have fun."

With *bises* all around, multiple thank yous and "we'll do this again soon," they went their separate ways, the young to go dancing, Stacey to find a hotel.

What a great evening! she thought. How long has it been since I've had so much fun?

She walked back toward the Seine, out of the office district, back to a more touristy area where she could find a hotel still open at this late hour. Easy enough to do in a city with over 7000 hotels to its claim.

There was one. A little decrepit, a little... how to say? seedier than what she was used to, but the light was on in the foyer and she could see someone behind the front desk.

Stacey walked in. "Hello," she said. "I'd like a room for the night. Do you have something available?"

He did. 85 Euros for the night. Payment in advance.

"Of course," replied Stacey, opening her handbag to get out her credit card as the clerk handed her a registration form and a pen.

Oh my God! To her astonishment, her wallet wasn't there. She opened her purse wider, rummaged through it, panicked, then plunked her purse on the front desk and started emptying it item by item. Hairbrush, house keys, Christophe's key, notebook, pen, car registration, make-up... It was all there except her wallet. And the credit cards *in* the wallet. *Merde! Merde! Merde!*

What could have happened? Did she leave it somewhere? Stacey's mind raced through her day, replaying all the events since she had left the house, then slowed down and stopped as she remembered window shopping with the girls and how, in the *Passage du Cerf*, another shopper had jostled her, even though the Passage wasn't crowded. That must be it! That must be when she lost her wallet!

"Do you have another means of payment?" asked the clerk. Stacey thought for a moment, then patted her pockets. There!

In her front pocket was the change she had put, absentmindedly, when they bought the picnic at the *épicerie*. She took the money out of her pocket and spread it out on the counter in front of her to count. Twenty, thirty, thirty euros in bills. Now the coins: six euros and 50 centimes.

She had a total of 36.50€.

"I can give you this now and then contact a friend in the morning for the rest," she proposed.

The clerk was having none of this. He had seen too many patrons sneak out without settling up. "Payment in advance. Only." He replied.

"Look, it's 36.50€. There's less than fifty euros missing."

"That's 45.50€ missing."

"I could leave you this," said Stacey, pointing to her wedding ring. "That will show you I'm coming back to settle up."

"What do you think this is? A pawn shop?"

Stacey felt defeated, no argument left in her. She gathered up her money, put it safely back in her pocket, then picked up her belongings and stowed them back in her handbag, before walking to the door.

"What am I going to do?" she murmured, more to herself than anything else.

The clerk, more gently, replied, "Why don't you just call your husband?"

That simple comment provoked a huge reaction, at least inwardly. In her mind, Stacey raged. What? Call her husband? You want me to call to the rescue the very reason I am here in the first place? You think ...

She said nothing, so the clerk continued. "Call your husband, he'll come and get you. I bet you'll work everything out before you even get home."

So what? Dr. Phil works the night shift now? Sure, calling her husband was such a simple solution. If she called him, he would drive in, then he would expect her to apologize for ignoring his calls, for disturbing him in the middle of the night, for .... The anger welled up in her. No way! No fxxking way would *she* apologize for her behavior to the man who was cheating and lying. To the man who had betrayed her. To the man who was still betraying her!

And this clerk! Her anger grew. What did he know of betrayal? Here he was smugly telling her what to do as if he knew everything. Had his girlfriend ever taken a secret lover? Did he ever learn that the person he trusted most had pissed on all his hopes and dreams? Here he was, giving her advice! She wanted to grab his shoulders and shake him until she shook all that certainty right out of him.

Stacey closed her eyes and took a deep breath, trying to control her anger.

The image of Stacey throwing her phone into the Seine appeared before her eyes. That great gust of freedom she had felt then now fell flat; she was dejected. If she hadn't thrown away the phone, she could use it to call one of her friends now. She thought back to the young man wearing the "mobilophobia" t-shirt. Perhaps he was right after all. Perhaps you should be afraid of a life *sans* mobile phone.

If she hadn't thrown her phone into the Seine, if she hadn't had all that fun with the girls, she'd have her wallet now and could pay for a hotel. Heck, she'd even have enough cash for a taxi home.

Her great gust of liberty was ending on a sour note.

The clerk yammered on about calling her husband, he'd seen many marital problems, yada, yada, yada. No longer paying any attention him, Stacey turned and left the hotel, dejected; wondering if this was really "the deal". Either she could play it safe, stay in a marriage which was comfortable and pleasant but based on cheating and lies, or she could live her life, have adventures... and risk sleeping on the street? Is this what life was trying to tell her?

14

Back to the bachelor pad

STACEY WALKED ON and on, because at this point, that was all she knew how to do. It was late. She was tired. She desperately needed sleep and had no means of paying for a hotel room.

By this time, most of Paris was dark. Even the restaurants and bars had closed. She walked back to the *Seine*, crossed the bridge to the *Ile de la Cité*, crossed another bridge to the left bank.

She saw herself again at the hotel. What a sorry sight

she had made, like a crazy woman, pulling everything out of her purse like that. That was so much stuff, yet nothing that would help her now.

Wait a minute, she thought, stopping in her tracks. She tried to focus. She had taken out her hairbrush, notebook, her keys.

And Christophe's key. She still had the key to Christophe's apartment in her purse.

She was saved!

She fished around in her handbag, verified that she did, indeed, have the key, then turned around and headed the other way, every step taking her close to Christophe's apartment and a bed where she could rest.

Some minutes later, Stacey felt tired but triumphant as she opened the door to Christophe's apartment. Despite her wallet being stolen, despite being kicked out of the hotel, she had found a solution. She was resourceful. She was...

Mortified.

There, in front of her, in Christophe's living room were Jean and Berenice, Jean wearing nothing but his boxers and socks (*Not a good look*, Stacey thought, *even if the socks were Ralph Lauren*), and Berenice in a negligée, possibly from *Tentation Lingérie*, the boutique Stacey had followed her to. Her arm was outstretched toward Jean, holding the lacey thong that Stacey had planted in the bed by the tips of her fingers. She looked angry, very angry.

The three stood there for a few seconds, frozen. Jean and Berenice looked at Stacey, Stacey looked back and forth between the two of them. This has been the furthest thing from her mind.

Jean spoke first, one of those stupid things people say without really thinking.

"You never called me back. Didn't you get my messages?" he asked. "I told you I'd come home late." As if that made what Stacey was seeing OK.

At the same time, Berenice's expression changed from anger to surprise. She turned toward Stacey. "I know you. I've seen you before..."

Before Berenice could say more, Stacey turned and ran. Out the door, down the four flights of stairs, into the night. She ran, crying, until she could run no more.

She was walking now, but her mind still raced. Whether she was ready for it or not, the confrontation had taken place. Jean knew that she knew; she would have to make a decision.

A car passed her on the street, the Clash blaring on the stereo despite the late hour, "Should I stay or should I go?"

Despite everything, Stacey chuckled. *More messages*

from the universe.

As her thoughts calmed, her tiredness returned. She really needed to find a place to stay. She walked on. And on.

15

Cinema

SUDDENLY, SHE saw a lighted façade a block or so down, a movie theater with an old-fashioned frontage, classic silver screen design with a neon line outlining the three-story marquee, the cinema's name in meter-high letters, movie billboards and the front door all lit up as well.

The front door was lit!

For Stacey, this was a godsend. She hurried down the street. At the box office inside the tiny foyer, she saw a small sign, "*Les Nuits du Champo.* Starting at midnight, three films + one breakfast. 15€"

Three movies for fifteen euros? She could afford it. She took a twenty bill from her pocket and handed it to the young woman tending the till.

"One, please."

"You've already missed the first movie."

"That's OK."

"Breakfast is only a croissant and coffee."

"That's OK," replied Stacey, a little more impatient this time. Now that she was close to a solution, she felt the fatigue of the day even more than before. Morpheus was doing more than reaching out for her; she was firmly in his grip. "That will suit me just fine. Can I have my ticket now?"

"Do you want some popcorn?" asked the young woman. "At this hour, I handle the refreshments counter, too."

This was too much. She was so close; she just had to get inside and this girl was blocking her way.

Inwardly, Stacey exploded. She was a volcano, erupting, sending its fire and lava on this girl who just wouldn't give her the ticket. She was a hurricane, blowing the girl out of her ticket window and off the face of the earth, the force of her winds screaming *Give me the ticket*. She was... a little off her rocker from weariness.

Stacey kept her calm and simply asked, "Can I get it with the 5€ you still owe me?"

"That's the price," smiled the girl.

"Ok then," said Stacey, skirting around the box office to the entrance doors, following the girl to the refreshment counter. She got her popcorn and her ticket and gratefully, finally, found her way into the darkened room where the credits were rolling at the end of the first movie.

In the demi-light flickering from the screen, Stacey noticed a handful of other movie-goers, scattered here and there throughout the room, which was a bit of a disappointment. The façade of the building was pure vintage and promised a "retro" experience. This viewing room, however, was modern; floors, walls and possibly ceiling (she couldn't see in the darkness) all covered in a deep blue carpet. A row of spotlights along each side wall created a pattern of light and shadow, making it appear that the walls were decorated with a shell pattern. It was attractive but mostly functional. The room itself was small, maybe 10 rows with six seats to the left and 3 seats to the right of the aisle, which made the silver screen (actually white) loom large at the front of the room. Again, Stacey felt a pang of disappointment that the silver screen was not silver, but *Le Champo* couldn't be held responsible for the incorrect English idiom. The seats, too, held disappointment. When the theater was built, they would have been covered in a rich, plush velour, probably red. Now, it was microfiber, surely functional but just not the same.

She took a seat off to the left, as far away from the other moviegoers as possible and settled in. She sat down and literally sank into the thick, comfortable cushions. It felt as if the chair was hugging her. The microfiber upholstery, too, was surprisingly soft to the touch. She would have to revise her preference for velour. After all the walking-- and playing and running and climbing!-- she had done that day, what a pleasure to relax in such a cozy seat. Stacey gave a sigh of contentment and munched on some popcorn as the house lights lowered and the next movie started.

It was *Lady Bird*, a semi-sweet story of a high school senior at a Catholic girls' school in Sacramento. She'd seen it before and had found it to be both touching and true to life. She settled in and watched the movie, but the late hour and the day's fatigue won out. She dozed off, then woke up here and there throughout the movie to see the scene where Lady Bird was in the principal's office and the principal (head nun? Principal nun? Stacey was so tired she couldn't think straight) told the young girl that it wouldn't be a bad thing if she wasn't able to go back east for college seeing how she loved Sacramento so much.

"I don't love Sacramento!" Lady Bird exclaimed.

"Yes you do," replied the nun. "The way you describe it in your application essay, it's clear that you love Sacramento."

"I don't love it," muttered the teenager. "I just pay attention."

"Well, isn't that the same thing?"

Stacey sat bolt upright. That small simple phrase hit her hard. If paying attention was the same as loving, then Jean did not love her. Stacey thought back to the telephone conversation she had overheard in which Jean told Berenice that Stacey was incapable of sending the DVD. He paid so little attention to her that he didn't see what she was capable of, neither the DVD nor all the rest. He didn't even notice how she had been neglecting the housework and the meals, how her habits had been erratic.

The kids had noticed. They had noticed and they had reacted, reaching out to her and expressing their concern. *That*, thought Stacey, *is love*.

The movie continued. Little by little Stacey relaxed again, drifting back into sleep.

When she woke again, it was *The Purple Rose of Cairo*. She loved that movie, a movie within a movie just like the book within a book genre she liked so much. Seeing it on the silver screen, in a darkened movie house, just like Mia

Farrow in the story... now, that was a treat.

She loved the scenes when Tom Baxter walks off the screen, when he and Cecilia, the Mia Farrow character, go to a restaurant and his movie money isn't accepted there, and when Tom takes Cecilia into movie land and the entire cast goes to the Copacabana. They sit at a table in the nightclub, sipping cocktails as the lovely Rita comes out to sing. In between her dozing, Stacey hears Rita croon, "Let's take it one day at a time."

The phrase caught in her brain. "Let's take it one day at a time." She had been worrying about her life, what to do about Jean's infidelity, how to help Laura and David finish their journey into adulthood, and here the answer came from the silver screen.

Stacey drifted off again to the nightclub singer's melodious strains, waking up again only after the third movie was finished, the house lights came on, and the young woman announced, "Ladies and gentlemen, coffee and croissants are being served in the foyer. We hope you enjoyed the films."

16

Church

STACEY HAD especially enjoyed the comfortable chair. She had slept well—just not long enough. After drinking the itsy bitsy cup of coffee, thinking an American mug would have been more to her liking, then nibbling on a lonely croissant, she left the movie theater.

Goodness! What time was it? She glanced at her watch. 5 am. *Aie*! Too early, especially after only a few hours of sleep. Stacey crossed the street then dragged her feet down the sidewalk, barely awake, barely standing she was so tired. What could she do? Where could she go? She followed the street along a small garden, dead-ending into some sort of mediaeval building. She found herself in front of a mock fortified wall, complete with crenels, protecting an inner courtyard and main building. Over the top of this battlement, she could see the steeply sloped slate roof of the main hall, the windows with stone fronts so highly sculpted they looked like lace, and an octagonal tower in the middle of the building. An actual tower! On any other day, Stacey would have stopped and admired this structure. Today, though, she was too tired. She barely glanced at it as she followed the street right, then left, then left again, bypassing the building and arriving at the Boulevard Saint Germain which she crossed, half jay-walking, half sleepwalking.

She stumbled on and found herself in front of a church with a big banner across the façade marked *Ouvre mes yeux*. "Open my eyes."

If I opened her eyes, I'd see an opportunity here, thought Stacey wryly, although the message was surely intended for loftier goals than finishing her night's sleep. Stacey pushed the door and entered the church.

It was beautiful.

Stacey paused a moment just inside the main door to admire the classic gothic architecture. One main nave, flanked by two smaller aisles on each side. In the main nave, the pillars started off on the ground, heavy and solid, then flew upward, growing narrower and finer until they interlaced high above, forming vaults as delicate as spider webs. The result was lofty, airy, pulling one upward toward God, making one want to be a better person.

At the far end of the church, Stacey could see the altar and the choir. Behind that were the lower arches and twisted pillars of the ambulatory, showcasing surprisingly modern stained glass windows. Stacey blinked, not believing her eyes. She looked up at the high windows near the ceiling. No, those were "normal," stained glass, that is, they looked like they were made in the same era as the rest of the church, exactly what you would expect to see. But below! She looked downward again. Modern, very modern, very blue. She hadn't known there were so many different shades of blue. Even at this distance, even in the low light of early morning, she could feel the whirlpools of color, moving slowly, one eddy disturbing another. She blinked, shook herself a little, and reminded herself that this is what happens when you get too tired. She took another look at the stained glass—the colors, the movement, it reminded her of Van Gogh's Starry Night. Her heart sang at the sheer beauty of it, then her practical side broke in, pushing her to go look for a place to "hole up."

She found the confessional, sat down in the small stall, shut the door behind her and settled in. The wooden bench was hard but the vertical walls were useful. She barely had to lean over to rest her cheek against the wall and close her eyes. *This probably isn't what they mean by "Let God support you," but it's working for me*, she thought as she dozed off.

She woke with a start some time later as a door opened close by and someone said softly in her ear, "Forgive me Father for I have sinned." Stacey didn't have the time to wonder what to do before her door opened, a kindly face smiled at her and said, much in the way you do on an airplane, "I think you're in my seat." Stacey blushed as the elderly man in the priest's collar offered his arm to help her out of the confessional. "If you're in need, we've got office hours which open in two hours. You can stay here until then." He gestured to the row of pews, then as he entered his side of the confessional, he winked at her and said "And if you have a need for confession, you know where to find me."

Did she feel a need for confession? Stacey stopped and thought for a moment. Wreaking havoc on her cheating husband and his fancy bit wasn't particularly mature but she didn't consider it to be a sin, much less something she would repent of. The kindly priest had asked her if she was in need—of anything. If she didn't repent for her vengeful actions, did she need anything else?

Pondering this, Stacey's eyes followed his gesture. She looked around the church and noticed the electric lights glowing high above in the triforium. They reminded her of Garrison Keillor's Father Wilber for whom the lights in the church were a protestant plot to take all the mystery out of religion. *Not here*, thought Stacey with a smile. Here, the lights were dim and were now supplemented by the morning light filtering through the stain glass, making the church barely lighter yet much more beautiful than when she had entered a few hours earlier. It was beautiful and peaceful here, a true sanctuary, a place where she felt at ease. What she really needed, though, was to decide what to do. A decision she, not the church, must make.

She turned to leave, out the heavily sculpted door, a few steps to cross the forecourt, into the sunlight, into the new day.

17

A new day

STACEY TURNED RIGHT, then right again onto a tiny street, the church on her right, gargoyles overhead, restaurant after restaurant on her left, all closed in the wee hours of the morning.

During meal times, the street would be hopping; now, though, it felt abandoned, derelict and sad. Stacey carried on, crossing a larger boulevard and coming to a fork in the road. A time for decisions, she said to herself, bemused that the physical world was mirroring her emotional world, and the universe just kept on sending messages.

She chose left, past a small ruin of a church, past more restaurants and cafés, Shakespeare and Company to the left, a park to her right and there, opposite her, the Seine. Stacey laughed to herself. She always looked to the Seine for comfort and here she was, without even meaning to.

She turned right on the Quai de Montebello, crossing *bouquiniste* after *bouquiniste*, the green boxes of the book vendors all firmly locked shut now. She didn't see the back side of *Notre Dame* or notice the majestic trees lining the sidewalk, so engrossed she was in her thoughts about the last month, since she had discovered Jean's infidelity, had tracked down the tart, and had tried to get revenge and create a breach between them.

Everyone liked the bad guys to be punished and she had tried to punish Jean and Berenice. She had sincerely tried her best. Stacey chuckled to herself, she had certainly shown creativity in this domain. She felt rather proud of herself, although she had only succeeded in creating minor irritation for them and had not really achieved anything. They were still together; they were still seeing one another.

Stacey thought, too, about Laura and David's intervention and how their relationship was so much better now. Laura had an artistic side which Stacey hadn't known. David, the geek, was more sensitive to peer pressure than she would have guessed. They were interesting people, and not just because they were her kids.

As she stopped for the light to change at the Pont Sully, a food truck passed. Stacey absent-mindedly read on its side "Stop dreaming, start doing." *Good advice*, she thought. She needed to take action. But what?

She crossed the street and walked down the embankment to be closer to the river instead of up on the sidewalk at street level. It was calmer here. The dominant sound was the sound of water lapping the concrete banks, the street traffic only a low murmur somewhere in the distance. She continued walking, always moving forward, her thoughts focusing themselves on the last twenty-four hours. Twenty-four hours in which she had lived a lifetime of experiences: her altercation with Madame Pipi, her talk with the homeless man in the bar, her wanderings in this beautiful city and the messages it had sent her, the craziness and fun with the girls.

How lucky to have met Corinne, Annie and Françoise! Although, now she thought about it, maybe she had created that luck because she had known to listen to Corinne and make her feel valued.

Jean had not made her feel valued. He did not pay attention to her. He had underestimated her. Maybe, though, she, Stacey, was partially to blame because she had underestimated herself as well. This month of researching, plotting, executing her plans had shown her she was very capable. Capable and adaptable. Those were important qualities.

She walked past the spot where the fly boats make a U-turn, which somehow made her feel she was entering unchartered territory, a point of no return. Here, river banks had been transformed into a concrete park. Along the shore line were a series of half circles, small concrete versions of a Roman amphitheater with the stage being the Seine. Stacey could imagine a zealous actor immersing himself too much in his role, taking one step too many backward and ploof! into the river. There were three or four amphitheaters interspersed with large, very modern sculptures and, to her right, on the slopes leading toward the street, more sculptures placed here and there in the landscaped gardens.

As Stacey continued walking, she remembered playing in the fountain, singing on the street, and climbing to the rooftop. She, Stacey, *quinquagennaire*, fifty-something, expat, housewife, had felt like the king of the world. She had dared. She had surpassed her limits—and she had had a ball! This last night, she had had the time of her life, and felt that so much more was possible. If she could climb the outside of a building, she could rock climb with David, and she could...

Her mind was buzzing with all that she now felt she could do.

Her thoughts were interrupted by a change in the sonorous background. The distant murmur of traffic and the sound of water lapping at the banks were drowned out by the click-clack of a train passing, first at a distance and now, as she approached the *Pont d'Austerlitz*, closer and closer. Its proximity jolted Stacey back to the present. She was here, in Paris, at dawn, 16.50€ in her pocket, no phone, no credit cards, a husband whom she loved despite his cheating, two kids whom she loved and who were almost grown up and would not need her very much longer.

What was she going to do?

First of all, she would cross the street. At a normal time of day, with a normal amount of traffic, that would have been a complicated task. It was a big intersection, complete with its own mini ring road, and pedestrians were supposed to cross in several steps. At 7 am, though, there wasn't a lot of traffic so Stacey did as the Parisians do. She jaywalked. She smiled to herself, noting yet another cultural difference. She continued walking along the quai. As she crossed at the next light, she happened to look left. There, in the distance, was the Gare de Lyon and its famous clock tower. Stacey was surprised. She hadn't realized she had come this far.

Funny choice of words, she thought, as she continued walking, the Seine and the sun as her guides.

Stacey realized that, with all these exciting new possibilities, with everything she had just discovered she was capable of, she had completely lost interest in Jean and Berenice, the illicit couple, in punishing them, splitting them up or even getting revenge. They just didn't matter.

She had completely lost interest in Jean, too. She loved him, but she would leave him, not out of moral justice nor hurt nor anger. She would leave Jean to his liaison, to his sordid little life, because a bigger life was waiting for her. A life of new experiences, new people, excitement, adventure. She hoped her future would be just like the last twenty-four hours: not always comfortable, maybe sleep deprived, but very, very interesting and worthwhile.

Stacey entered a new neighborhood, new in that she had changed from one neighborhood to the next, and also new in that it was being completely rebuilt, completely revitalized. Building after building had been torn down, the traditional stone, brick and stucco now replaced by glass and steel. Stacey could see streets—actual streets with official street signs—which were staircases, impossible to drive on with a car. Office and apartment buildings were built using the natural slope of the terrain, creating new perspectives, new ways of living. Here, a clunky "big box store" on the ground level was topped by two high rises in green glass, each floor jutting out at a different, improbable angle, the result oddly harmonious.

The neighborhood was still under construction so Stacey was not surprised when she crossed a construction worker on his way to his building site, his t-shirt commanding "Break all the rules." *Hmm*, thought Stacey. She had broken a few already this past night. She had enjoyed it, too.

A few minutes later, a woman walking her dog, a cute ball of fluff, came toward Stacey. As they reached one another, Stacey could see emblazoned across her shirt "Create the life you want to live." Could it really be that simple?

She had just decided she did not want Jean nor the Jean and Berenice duo in her life. Maybe that was the real reason she had chucked her phone into the Seine? She was throwing Jean and Berenice into the river, too. She wanted them out.

But what did she want *in* her life? Her kids, of course. What else? Her mind raced as she thought of everyone and everything she loved, the experiences she wanted to have, and what she wanted in her new life.

Suddenly, on the streetlight right at eye level, Stacey saw a white piece of paper. Someone had drawn the head and shoulders of a woman surrounded by a ring of faces: some children, some men, some women. At the top, in a lovely cursive, were the words "You are beautiful." In English. Not French.

Stacey smiled to herself. She was beautiful. The universe, and the piece of A4 paper, told her so.

She crossed the street and walked up the stairs to the esplanade of the *Bibliothèque Nationale.* Stacey had seen the library from the car window without ever actually stopping to visit, so she took a moment now to wander around. Four buildings, shaped like upended books stood in the four corners of the rectangular esplanade. In the middle was a hole, also rectangular, opening up onto a garden, no, a mini forest, a surprisingly dense swath of trees. At the edge of the "forest," a floor below, she could see study rooms underneath the esplanade, little cubicles opening up to foliage and sunlight. How nice it must be to work there! She would have to try it. She could also try...

Stacey walked around all four sides of the esplanade, thinking of all the things she could try, thinking of the life she now wanted to create. She passed by a couple practicing ballroom dancing, the woman swooping and twirling in her partner's guiding arms. *Ooooooh, I'd like to try that.*

Further on was an entire troupe of dancers, clearly amateurs, getting a little extra practice before the workday started. They performed a complicated choreography, an unusual mix of Chinese traditional dance and Bollywood. With maracas. It was... unusual, yes, that was the best word, but the people were clearly having fun and enjoying being together as a group. *That would be fun to try, too.*

Stacey continued on. A runner passed by. A skateboarder did tricks. She had never imagined so many people would be outside living their passions this early in the morning. As she reached the third side of the esplanade, she came to a virtual reality lab, its sign proclaiming

"Le monde a changé. Venez l'essayer."

The world has changed, come try it.

Stacey smiled. The universe was still sending her messages.

She rounded the corner to the fourth side and thought *Trees in prison.* She saw row after row of planting boxes, raised beds planted with trees too close together, all scrupulously staying within the space allotted them by vertical bars. It was unnatural. It was cruel. Trees were meant to grow freely, to take root and reach for the stars, not to be pruned into something smaller, something... submissive. She shook her head in dismay.

Why was she getting so upset about this? What was she? Some sort of trees' rights activist? Or did the trees remind her of herself, of how she had lived all these years. What was that t-shirt she had seen yesterday? "Inside each woman is a wild thing, let her out." She now knew that that was true.

Stacey turned the last corner, back to the side facing the Seine. She sat down on the edge of the esplanade, feet on the steps below, and thought again (or more? for she had never really stopped thinking about it) of her decision to leave Jean.

It was a big risk, scarily big, but she knew Laura and David would be there to help her, just as she would continue to help them. They had shown her recently what they were made of and she had no worries. They would be fine. They would all be fine.

Her eyes followed the Seine to the left, back toward the city center from where she had come, then to the right, an area she didn't know, where the sun was rising, casting its rosy glow.

Just then, a small delivery van drove by. Stacey had just enough time to see the fancy detailing on its side panel, *En route pour l'aventure.* Head for adventure.

Stacey took a deep breath and smiled.

She knew what she was going to do and her future would be just as rosy as the sunrise over Paris that morning.

Acknowledgments

I am lucky to have good friends who helped me at all the different stages of writing and editing this novel. Some gave input here and there while others read and reread the many versions, helping me improve with each iteration. All of them went above and beyond the duties of friendship.

Thank you to Stephanie Strong, Tony Maiorino, Christa Lewis, Robin Mosley, Jennifer Strand, Jean-Louis Oszvath, Loïc Cahierre, Eve Lindemuth and Anne P. for all your help and support.

Thanks also to Lindsay Guzzardo, my editor, who was very patient while she coaxed me through a major rewrite.

About the Author

Carolyn Eychenne is an author of fiction and non-fiction works. *Sunrise over Paris* is her first novel but not the first book she has published, the other being a French-language book about digital platforms. While radically different and a lot less fun, it led her back to her true love, writing.

Not quite "an American in Paris," Carolyn Eychenne has lived most of her adult life in the suburbs of Paris, after growing up in southern California. Even after so many years abroad, she is still fascinated by the cultural differences. And the food. She especially enjoyed doing all the hands-on research (hiking and dining) for *Sunrise over Paris*.

www.carolyneychenne.com

Photo: Vincent Hoe

10.30
2.00

Printed in Great Britain
by Amazon

47702403R00162